THE ALPHABETICAL HOOKUP LIST

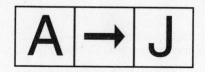

A → J

Phoebe McPhee

POCKET BOOKS

New York   London   Toronto   Sydney   Singapore

An *Original* Publication of MTV Books/Pocket Books

POCKET BOOKS, a division of Simon & Schuster Inc.
1230 Avenue of the Americas, New York, NY 10020

Copyright © 2002 by 17th Street Productions, an Alloy, Inc. Company, and One Ear Productions

 Produced by 17th Street Productions,
an Alloy, Inc. company
151 West 26th Street
New York, NY 10001

MTV Music Television and all related titles, logos, and characters are trademarks of MTV Networks, a division of Viacom International Inc.

Library of Congress Cataloging-in-Publication Data: 2002104579

ISBN: 0-7434-4842-1

First MTV Books/Pocket Books trade paperback printing July 2002

10 9 8 7 6 5 4 3 2 1

POCKET and colophon are registered trademarks of Simon & Schuster Inc.

Cover design by Amy Beadle
Printed in the U.S.A.

For information regarding special discounts for bulk purchases, please contact
Simon & Schuster Special Sales at 1-800-456-6798 or business@simonandschuster.com

For Brandon

Jodi Stein pulled her brand-new silver Volkswagen Beetle over to the side of the road just outside the Pollard University campus.

This is it, she thought. *"Today is the first day of the rest of your life."*

She'd seen that once on a bumper sticker on the Long Island Expressway and had always thought it was cute.

Jodi allowed herself a little smile in the rearview mirror. Even after twelve hours of driving, she had to admit she looked pretty fine. No, make that *very* fine. It hadn't been easy to choose an outfit, either. What could you possibly wear for a twelve-hour drive from Great Neck to the heart of Georgia—and still dazzle your future Kappa Kappa Gamma sorority sisters upon your arrival?

The answer: school-spirit casual.

Specifically, this style consisted of yellow satin gym shorts (not too showy, and a colorist had once told Jodi that yellow complemented her sandy brown hair), a green PU sweatshirt

(Jodi always tried to wear a little green to bring out the green flecks in her hazel eyes, and wouldn't you know it—green was one of PU's school colors!), and tennis socks with pompoms on them. Oh, and of course her gold charm necklace—the one with a namesake pendant. The one Buster had given her to mark their first anniversary, almost a year ago to the day.

"Hey, Buster, can you believe it?" Jodi whispered. "In less than a week we'll have been together—I mean, like, *officially* together—for two whole years."

Buster didn't answer. He had been asleep since they'd stopped at Denny's, despite the fact that he'd slurped down three coffee milk shakes.[1]

She watched him in the passenger seat, passed out in his little sugar coma. Curled up like that, he looked even cuter than usual. His square-jawed, close-cropped blond head lolled to one side, and his perfectly sculpted body was completely relaxed. Jodi loved the way Buster looked. She especially loved his powerful neck. Some girls loved guys with long, skinny necks. But those kinds of girls usually had pierced tongues and smoked too much and spent all their time in dark clubs where being cool depended on how depressed you looked. The chest, though: that was really what mattered. And Buster had chest from here to Kalamazoo.

"Buster?" she tried again.

□□□□□□□□□□□□□□□□□□□□□□□□□□□□□□
1 Best cure for a hangover.

Still no answer.

They had driven together all the way from Long Island, playing that alphabet game where you have to locate letters of the alphabet in signs and license plates in order from *A* to *Z*. It hadn't exactly been the most romantic trip in the world. But they had made it, and there was nothing more romantic than the fact that they were going to college together. It was what they had always planned. Getting accepted to the same school, living apart in dorms freshman year so they could each have the true college experience, and then getting an apartment together sophomore year. . . .

But she was getting ahead of herself. They hadn't even driven into the campus parking lot. She was excited. And nervous. And unable to keep still. She couldn't wait any longer. She *had* to wake up Buster so they could both always remember this moment.

"Psst! Buster." She leaned over and rubbed his chest. Do I Look Like a Fucking People Person? was written on his T-shirt in big black letters. His crutches—he had broken his leg in two places at the fifth we're-going-to-college party—were lying across both of their laps. His cast had been signed by all of their friends, but Jodi couldn't help but notice a few girls' names she had never heard of. Come to think of it, that cast had more girls' signatures on it than the wall of the girls' locker room at Great Neck High School. Then again, that was no surprise. Lots of girls loved Buster. Who wouldn't? Buster had always been a charmer—but his heart belonged solely to Jodi Stein. And it always would, no matter how many ditzy girls signed his cast. He had placed a Pollard University sticker over *Good luck in college! We love you, Mom and Dad.*

"What are you doing?" Buster mumbled, opening his eyes. "Why'd you stop? Are we in Georgia yet?"

"We're here. I mean it's *right there.* Pollard University. Our college. See that red brick building right on the other side of the gate? That's a dorm, Buster! Can you believe it? We're in *college.* And in less than a week we'll have been together for—"

"Oh God, I hate when you get like this."

Jodi smiled. "Like what?"

"Like all nostalgic and shit. Like when you force us to stop everything we're doing and appreciate the moment." He yawned, then burped.

Jodi stopped smiling. "But Buster, come on. This is special."

"Will you drive? I gotta piss."

"Please don't go in a cup again," Jodi gently chided.

"So keep driving. Then I won't have to."

Jodi stepped on the gas and drove through the gate into the parking lot. Buster opened the door, slid his crutches out first, then eased himself up. Struggling to keep his balance, he pissed in a satisfying puddle on the concrete. Jodi glanced anxiously in every direction. They were less than thirty feet from the front door of Maize Hall, their dorm and home for the next nine months. Luckily the parking lot was deserted. Okay. No need to panic. She figured she could forgive this one little disgusting display. After all, the poor guy was on crutches.

"Look, Jodi, honey," Buster said, in a high, dreamy voice. "It's my first leak as a college man. I'm so glad you were here to share it with me. We'll always remember it. One day we'll tell our grandchildren all about it."

"Okay, very funny," Jodi muttered. "Now put it away."

Buster zipped up his pants and frowned at the dorm. "This is it? It looks like a fucking prison."

Jodi shrugged. True, Maize Hall wasn't very impressive. It was one of the newer dorms, pretty much just a big red cube. But most of the buildings on the PU campus were beautiful. There were even real old southern mansions from the early nineteenth century. Several Confederate generals had been educated right here. It was *historic.*

"Man," Buster muttered. "I knew I should have . . ." His voice trailed off.

A girl walked out of Maize Hall. She looked exactly like a young Pamela Anderson—at least, as far as Jodi was concerned. She was wearing cutoff shorts and a bikini top. She froze when she saw Buster.

"Oh, you *poor thing!*" she exclaimed. "A broken leg!"

Jodi scowled at her.

Buster grinned. "It's not a big deal," he said sheepishly.

The girl burst out laughing.

"What's so funny?" Jodi demanded.

"That shirt!" She pointed right at Buster's thick chest. "That shirt!" She shook her head, then cupped her hand over her mouth. "Oops! I forgot something." She disappeared back inside, but not before wagging her boobs at Buster and giving him a big, toothy smile.

"Whoa," Buster murmured. He accidentally stepped in his own piss with his good foot.

"What?" Jodi spat.

He grinned at her across the roof of the car. "I love college. I love college! I LOVE COLLEGE!" He hobbled toward the front door.

Jodi was left standing in the parking lot.

She couldn't help but remember when her family had adopted a Tibetan terrier from the North Shore Animal League on Long Island and brought him to their big house for the first time. The dog had pissed, then chased after everybody—just like Buster was doing now.

Well, Buster, Jodi thought. *You sure look like a fucking people person now.*

She took a deep breath. She was not about to let Buster's lame behavior ruin her first day on campus. Clearly he was just as anxious and overwhelmed as she was, and this was how he was choosing to deal with it. Fine. He'd stop acting like such a shitbag as soon as they settled in and got used to the place. After all, he'd been an asshole when they were applying to colleges, too. Nervousness brought out the child in him. But PU would cure him of his immaturity.

Jodi grabbed her big overnight bag and followed in Buster's limping footsteps. Maize Hall had been featured on the virtual on-line tour she took of Pollard, so she knew the floors of the dorm were made up mostly of sets of triples. There was a shared bathroom between them and a few singles on each end of the hall. Maize had actually been her last choice when she'd filled out the housing form because it was supposed to be the artsy dorm—but that's where she had been assigned. It would be fine, though, since she would have her own room. Jodi had requested a single. She wanted the full college experience, but she didn't want the *full* full college experience.

Sure, she liked the *idea* of roommates—friends made and cherished for life—but as an only child she didn't really think she could sleep with someone breathing next to her. Unless of course it was Buster and they had just had amazing sex. Anyway, soon she would pledge Kappa Kappa Gamma, and her sorority sisters would be her cherished-for-life-type friends, so it didn't really matter.

The first thing Jodi saw when she walked through the doors was a fat girl slumped behind a desk. Buster was already gone.

The girl was sound asleep, with enormous glasses propped on top of her head. She had about fifty name tags stuck all over her entire body, covering her clothes and arms and legs. The only one that wasn't obscene and was in the proper name tag position said, *Hello, my name is . . . K. J. Martin.* The other name tags said, among other things, *Hello, my name is . . . Lazy-Eyed Narcoleptic K. J. Martin; Hello, my name is . . . Wake me up if I lose any weight; Hello, my name is . . . For hot sex, please leave your name and room number here;*

Hello, my name is . . . Laura, Come meet us at Tanked Bar or call me on my cell, Tina.

The name tag stuck to her forehead said, *FYI: This is my ass, not my face,* and the one pressed over her mouth said, *Blow me.*

Jodi was a little taken aback. She wasn't sure what to do. She had never seen a human bulletin board before.

"Uh, excuse me," she said.

The lazy-eyed, narcoleptic K. J. Martin person didn't wake up.

"Uh, hello."

There was a terrifying nose snort and lazy-eyed, narcoleptic K. J. Martin sat straight up in her chair. She struggled to speak for a second. Then she ripped the name tag off her mouth, said, "Ow," and then said, "Hi," as if all this was completely normal and had happened a thousand times before.

Jodi tried to smile. "Hi, I'm Jodi Stein. I just arrived."

"No, you just left," lazy-eyed, narcoleptic K. J. Martin said sarcastically.

Jodi's forehead wrinkled. "Um . . . I just need my room assignment," she said. She didn't want to get angry, but for somebody covered in stickers, this girl was unbelievably obnoxious. Jodi just wanted to get to her room as soon as possible. Especially as it was becoming a distinct possibility that she would become hypnotized by lazy-eyed, narcoleptic K. J. Martin's traveling left eyeball. It floated from side to side. It was impossible not to stare at it.

Lazy-eyed, narcoleptic K. J. Martin touched the side of her cheek and then ripped the name tag off it. "Ow," she said, looking at it. On it was a picture of a jagged scar. "Ha ha, very funny," she said. The person who had drawn the scar on the name tag had also drawn one directly on the cheek itself. "Now, what's your name?"

"Jodi Stein," Jodi said again. "I'm in a single."

"Yeah, right, I'm *so* sure of *that*," lazy-eyed, narcoleptic K. J. Martin said.

"I had a lot of boxes shipped here," Jodi said. "They're supposed to be waiting for me in my room."

Lazy-eyed, narcoleptic K. J. Martin looked down at a list of names and room numbers. Suddenly she got upset. "Oh my God. Where are my glasses? They stole my glasses again!"

"They're on top of your head," Jodi said.

Lazy-eyed, narcoleptic K. J. Martin felt the top of her head very tentatively, found the glasses, and put them on. Her eye still wandered around behind the lens. They were the worst kind of glasses, the big round upside-down kind that makes anyone who wears them look like a scary insect.

"Stein, Stein," she said, looking down at the list. "Here it is: Stein, Josi. Room 213. Oh, we're next-door neighbors, Josi."

"It's Jo*di*," Jodi said.

"Well, actually, it says here that your name is Josi," lazy-eyed, narcoleptic K. J. Martin said, referring again to the list. There was one blank name tag left, and she wrote *Josi Stein* on it and handed it to Jodi. "Josi, you're one flight . . ." Suddenly she was slumped over asleep again.

Jodi peeled the paper backing off the *Hello, my name is . . . Josi Stein* name tag, stuck it on the back of lazy-eyed, narco-leptic K. J. Martin's head, and went upstairs to find her single.[2]

She paused when she got to room 213. Something was wrong here. It was in the middle of the hall, where the triples were, instead of at the end of the hall. She unlocked the door and found herself staring at a room with three beds in it. No way. She panicked for a moment: *Shit! Shit! Shit!* Hadn't anyone read her housing questionnaire? When she'd checked *single,* she'd meant she wanted to live in one, not that she *was* one. . . .

But then she realized what was really going on and instantly relaxed. *Daddy.* Of course. He had obviously done this for her. He had paid triple housing fees so she could have a bigger room. Just because they had put her in a triple didn't mean she would actually have two roommates. When she'd left home this morning—right at the crack of dawn—he'd wished her luck and said she was in for a big surprise.

And this was it.

Her own triple. It was so cool. She had three times as much shelf and closet space, and she could push two of the beds together to make a double. Or she could find a way to get rid of the beds altogether and buy a queen-size bed. She was really going to make the place look great. She surveyed her estate. Well . . . actually, it was pretty small. It was

---

2 Incidentally, lazy-eyed, narcoleptic K. J. Martin was wearing the exact same outfit as Jodi—a fact that Jodi chose to ignore.

smaller than her room at home. If the triples were this small, she couldn't imagine what a single would be like. How could three people survive in a room like this? She couldn't wait for Buster to see it.

The first thing she took out of her bag was the picture of her and Buster at prom. It was in a silver Tiffany frame, engraved with their initials—J. S. and B. N. She placed it on one of her three desks. This would be her picture desk. Perfect. Soon it would be filled with all her cherished memories of college, too: beer bongs with her Kappa Kappa Gamma sisters, her first official "college" date with Buster. . . . Well, she knew what she had to do once she got all unpacked. She had to go buy lots of picture frames.

2

"Jib, Carla, that's enough," Celeste Alexander told her overly enthusiastic parents.[3] "I can take it from here."

The Alexander family (or "tribe," as Jib referred to it) had just unloaded the last of Celeste's bags and boxes from their rental car. It was strange for Celeste to see all of her belongings on the pavement outside of Maize Hall. To be honest, it was kind of embarrassing. The corner of her white down comforter stuck out of one of her duffel bags. She blushed as if her bras and panties were on display and not a tiny corner of a comforter. But it was her *bedding,* for God's sake, and anything that went on her *bed* was personal and private and didn't have to be flown proudly from the campus flagpole.

Far more embarrassing, however, were Jib and Carla. Not that this was anything new.

As always, Celeste had tried to disassociate herself as much as possible from the two of them. She'd started with her

---

3 Both of Celeste's parents insisted on being called by the names they'd been given while living on a Marin County commune during the summer of 1972.

wardrobe. She'd chosen a red plaid jumper. True, it made her look like she was in the seventh grade, but she really didn't care. It was the exact opposite of Carla's batik-print south-western-style dress—or robe, or muumuu, or whatever it was.

Jib, as usual, was wearing a too-bright and too-tight tie-dye.

They looked like college freshmen. Carla was draped with enough beads and necklaces and bracelets to sink a ship. *Jesus.* Celeste bowed her head. Her long brown curls hung in her face. She should have cut off her hair, too. That was the Alexander tribe giveaway. Celeste's hair was exactly the same length and shade of brown as both Carla's and Jib's—only without the streaks of gray.

"You guys can go now," Celeste whispered. "Seriously."

"Don't be ridiculous," Jib said. His breath still reeked from the joint he'd smoked in the car. "I'm going to carry every single one of these bags and boxes upstairs and help you unpack and settle in." He coughed, then grabbed a Healthy Treasures shopping bag. It was filled with fifty different things made out of tofu and small cartons of soy milk. "And remember: Just because you're in college doesn't mean you have to eat shit and get cancer."

"Right," Celeste mumbled. She had every intention of throwing the whole bag out as soon as he left and eating the first bacon cheeseburger she could find.

At least she had requested a single. That meant she wouldn't have to start introducing her parents to everybody. On the other hand, she *could* use some help with her stuff. She had brought all her books, carefully packing them in alphabetical order and labeling the boxes: *Aristotle–Camus, Albert. Chekhov, Anton–Flaubert, Gustave. Sade, Marquis de–Shakespeare, William.* There were at least a dozen of them. She had an entire box filled only with Sartre and books about Sartre.

Jib paused at the dorm entrance. "You know, a great swami once told me that some people can eat shit and turn it into gold," he mused, unfortunately out loud. "Some people can eat gold and turn it into shit. It's up to us to decide which one we'll be."

"But Jib, baby," Carla said, hoisting a box into her arms. "Don't all people turn whatever they eat into shit eventually? Isn't that what's commonly known as the digestive system? Our sweetheart knows that." She winked at Celeste. "Ashes to ashes, dust to dust, that kind of thing, right? It's science."

"Hmmm, heavy," Jib said, nodding.

Celeste didn't know what he was calling "heavy"—her mom's nonsensical comment or the bag of food—but she didn't really care either way. She just wanted to get upstairs and start her life as a college student. Jib and Carla had been acting strange ever since they'd left Manhattan. They kept referring to Celeste in the third person and giving her all kinds of weird advice, as if she were four years old. Jib was the worst, though. He'd made all these sighing sounds, and his eyes had been teary the whole ride. (Then again, he'd been smoking, and the car *was* pretty cloudy.) He'd even insisted on buying Celeste something at a Howard Johnson's gift shop when they'd stopped for gas. The only thing Celeste had seen that might be remotely useful in college was a Maryland Is for Lovers shot glass—and she didn't want it. "Come on, I want to buy my little girl something," Jib had insisted. Finally, just to shut him up and get the hell out of there, she'd chosen a cinnamon-apple granola bar.

Oh, well. Maybe her parents were feeling nostalgic for their own college days. Celeste supposed she could relate. Maybe *she* would feel nostalgic about college one day, too. She took a moment to look up at Maize Hall. (It was named Maize because the campus, built in 1853, was on some former Native American territory. Celeste knew everything about the university because she had studied all the orientation materials very carefully.)

She had actually requested a different dorm. Maize was known as a party dorm, and she had wanted to be in Abbey, which had once been a nuns' convent. But Maize was nice enough. As long as she was in her own room—where she could study and organize her things precisely the way she wanted them—it didn't really matter where she lived. It was peaceful here, quiet. The campus was filled with beautiful trees, green and lush and still. And there were actual peach trees! You could just go over and pick a peach. That was something you didn't see on Eighty-third and Riverside Drive. She knew she would like it here. It had a great "aura," as Jib would say.

Celeste picked up her box labeled *Saints, Biographies of,* and almost dropped it when a gorgeous guy in a jean jacket walked by and smiled at her. That particular box was sealed with about fifty layers of tape because she had hidden the *Kama Sutra* in the book jacket of a biography of Saint Lucia.

"He's cute," Carla whispered. She giggled. "Doesn't our little honey want to say hello?"

On second thought, maybe Celeste *could* handle all the luggage herself. She'd just make several trips. She put the box back down.

"Hey, Carla? Jib?" Celeste forced a smile. "Thanks a lot for driving me all the way down and everything, but I can take it from here."

Carla and Jib exchanged a glance.

"Well, okay, then," Carla said. "Jib, our angel wants to handle the rest herself."

For a moment Jib just stared at Carla. It looked as though he hadn't understood her. The pot had slowed his response time. Finally he nodded and walked back to the car.

Weirdly enough, Celeste felt a little lump in her throat. The way her parents were standing there, with those stoned smiles on their faces . . . well, it reminded her of home. She rushed forward to embrace both of them in one big Alexander tribe hug.

"Don't forget why our sweet pea was named Celeste," Carla murmured.

"Because she came straight from the heavens," Jib breathed.

Celeste rolled her eyes. The lump receded. This was what happened when your mother was an ex-nun turned social worker and your father was an ex–Buddhist monk who now devoted his whole life to Zen asceticism (except for the celibacy and no-drugs part)—and you were conceived on a mountain near Woodstock, New York.

"Now, listen, Jib, Carla," Celeste said, pulling away from them. "I want you to drive safely. Don't forget to lock the front door at night. And don't use the stove to light joints. Use a match. Come to think of it, it's time to change the fire detector battery and—"

"Our baby is so worried," her mother interrupted. "Isn't that sweet?"

"So sweet," Jib agreed.

After another quick squeeze Jib and Carla got back into their rental car. Celeste grabbed her box of *Saints, Biographies of* and walked into Maize, blissfully alone.

No one was at the desk, but there was a list of names and room numbers, so Celeste looked up her own room number. Luckily she was on the second floor. Room 213. It wouldn't be hard at all to carry all her stuff up here. Not at all. This was it! She was alone, at college—on her own, for the first time ever in her entire life. She was an *adult*.

She raced upstairs and threw open the door—then froze.

A girl was sitting on one of the beds.

3

"Oh, sorry, I must be in the wrong room," Celeste said, ducking back out to look at the room number again.

"No problem," Jodi said. She took her new leather Filofax out of her bag and wrote *have lock installed* in the things-to-do section. Thank God she didn't have roommates. She would hate to live with that freak. *Saints, biographies of?* And what was up with all that plaid? Who actually wore a red plaid schoolgirl's outfit to college? FI[4]: This girl had never been laid. She'd never even come close.

Celeste walked back inside. "Actually, I'm supposed to be here," she said. She glanced around the room. There were three single beds, but for some reason, they were all pushed together to form one big bed against one wall. That was so strange. Celeste had heard that there was a lot of sexual experimentation in college—wild Greek orgies, girls fooling around with other girls—but she

□□□□□□□□□□□□□□□□□□□□□□□□□□□□□□□

4 First impression.

hadn't thought it happened in the dorms before classes had even *started.*

"There must be a mistake," Jodi said. "I think I'm supposed to have my own room."

Thank God, Celeste thought. She hadn't slept with a guy yet, so she certainly had no intention of sleeping with a girl. And even if she *did,* it definitely wouldn't be this girl. First of all, this girl (whoever she was) was in Celeste's room. Second, Celeste already knew she was exactly the kind of girl she couldn't stand. She was wearing yellow satin gym shorts and a green Pollard U sweatshirt and had tennis socks with pom-poms on them. She had hazel eyes with a little green in them—and Celeste knew she was just the type who always wore green to try to make her eyes appear greener than they really were. She had long, shaggy sandy brown hair in a bunchy ponytail and actually had one of those gold necklaces around her neck with her name on it in script letters. Celeste wasn't close enough to read the name, but she would bet on Saint Joan's ashes that it ended with an *i.* She would also bet that there was a perfect back-to-school pedicure under those tennis socks. The girl was tall, with big, muscular legs.

"I'm supposed to have my own room, too," Celeste said. She frowned. "At least, I think I am. . . ."

Suddenly Jodi realized what might have happened. She was in the wrong room. She was in *Josi* Stein's room. This whole thing was a misunderstanding. Any minute Josi Stein would walk in and claim her room and her new roommate, and Jodi would go to the housing department and find her single. Actually, a fresh-man on campus with such a similar name would probably cause Jodi a lot of problems with registration and stuff—so the sooner they alerted the administration, the better.

"You know, I just realized *I'm* probably the one in the wrong room," Jodi said. She flashed a fake smile.

Celeste breathed a sigh of relief and smiled back at her. "Oh. Good. I'm sorry about the mix-up." She put her box of books on the desk in front of the window. "Anyway, I'm going to go down and get more of my stuff." She had turned to leave the room when the door opened.

A girl walked in. She was followed by a miserable-looking, gray-haired man who was either her father or her grandfather. Or maybe he was just her valet. He was dressed in a dark suit—but he was stooped and sweaty, dragging two enormous army duffel bags behind him.

Celeste blinked. She herself might look like a seventh grader, but this new girl was actually wearing pigtails. Long black ones. They matched the color of her eyes and her T-shirt, which said Porn Star. And she had a nose ring. And her pants looked like they were made of rubber. So did her thick lips. They were painted purple.

"Oh, hey, y'all," the girl said, eyeing both Celeste and Jodi up and down. She spoke with a southern twang. "So much for getting a single, huh? Dudes, why do they even bother sending us those housing request forms?" She laughed and threw her hands above her head. "Fascist pigs! Just kidding."

Jodi gaped at her.[5]

"I'm Alison Sheppard," the girl said. "You can call me Ali. Pleased to meet you."

"Uh . . . I—I'm Celeste," Celeste stammered. *And I'm not going to call you anything because this isn't your room.*

"I'm Jodi," Jodi said.

"Y'all from up north?" Ali asked.

The gray-haired man cleared his throat.

Celeste and Jodi glanced at each other.

"I'm from New York," Celeste said.

"Really?" Ali's dark eyes brightened. "My boyfriend goes to NYU. He's a DJ. I'm from Atlanta. It's only an hour away. You know, y'all can—"

The man cleared his throat again. Ali frowned at him.

"I have to leave," he said.

"Why?" she muttered. "Is your girlfriend waiting for you?"

His craggy face darkened. "I thought we weren't going to get into all that right now," he said.

"Whatever, dude. If you want to leave, just leave."

"My name is Dad," he said. "Not Dude."

Ali raised her eyebrows.

"Well. Have a nice time at college," he said. He gave her an awkward pat on the back. She didn't react. With that, he stomped out of the room.

Jodi and Celeste looked at each other again.

Ali shrugged. "Me and my dad have a terrible relationship,"

□□□□□□□□□□□□□□□□□□□□□□□□□□□□□□□□

5 FI: Techno meets the KKK meets . . . *my worst nightmare.* Dudes?! Y'all?! Who *talks* like that?

she said. "He left my mom for our interior decorator when I was ten years old. But hey, show me the teenage girl who has a good relationship with her father, and I'll show you a hog that flies. Ha!" She laughed again, then pulled a lollipop out of her pocket.

A hog that flies? Celeste and Jodi both wondered.

"I have a good relationship with my father," Jodi said, pursing her lips.

Sure, you do, Ali thought. She took a look around the room as she unwrapped the lollipop. It was funny. She'd always imagined that college would introduce her to all sorts of new, exciting, interesting people—unlike high school, where for four long years she'd scoured the halls for new, exciting, interesting people but could never quite manage to find any. High school had been a yawn-o-rama. The problem was, she'd never locked into any kind of *scene.* And she'd tried. Lord, how she'd tried. She'd done the cheerleader thing. She'd done the punk thing, the goth thing, the reclusive artist thing (although it was kind of hard to find a scene if you were all by yourself) . . . and finally, thanks to her new boyfriend, Sensei, she'd settled into the trip-hop hypnotica thing. It wasn't bad, but she'd honestly thought that college would free her from all that searching. Unfortunately, judging from the looks of these two . . .

Ali sucked on the lollipop. Whatever. Pollard was a big place. There were plenty of people out there. Plenty of scenes. She wouldn't have to look that hard. Her eyes settled on the three beds pushed together.

THE ALPHABETICAL HOOKUP LIST

"Look, y'all, I requested a single," she said. "Obviously it didn't work out that way. Which figures. Freshmen never get what they want. And I'm willing to make the best of it, but this is ridiculous. I mean, I'm all for closeness, but not this much closeness. I'd hate to be in the middle of this sandwich. Know what I'm saying?"

Jodi swallowed. A very, very unpleasant idea was creeping into her mind. *There isn't any Josi Stein.* It was a mistake. A typo. She'd taken a typing course last summer back home in Great Neck—at Daddy's insistence ("She might as well know how to type if she's going to be writing term papers and the like.")—so she knew very well that the *S* key was right next to the *D* key. And if there wasn't any Josi Stein, then . . .

"I requested a single, too," Celeste said.

Jodi's eyes darted between the two of them. Her face turned pale. "Why am I starting to get the feeling that everybody in this room requested a single?" she asked.

"Not me, I requested a triple."

The girls turned.

It was Buster. He was standing at the door. He hobbled into the room on his crutches and looked at the beds. "Cool. I'm just in time for a ménage à roommate."[6]

"Who are *you?*" Ali drawled.

"Don't you knock?" Celeste demanded. She took one look at this cretin and instantly felt ill. Judging from that confident smirk, he obviously thought he was God's gift to women. And

6 FI: Make that more than cool. The chick in the plaid is a hottie, even if her tits aren't that big, but the spooky chick with the pigtails is an even hotter hottie.

maybe he was, if you liked beefy morons who looked like they'd just walked off the set of a sporting goods store commercial. Not to mention that ridiculous T-shirt. *Do I look like a fucking people person?* The answer, in a word: NO.

"Sorry," Buster said sweetly.

"Everyone, this is my boyfriend, Buster," Jodi said. "Hi, honey. This is . . ." She hadn't even bothered to remember their names.

"Ali Sheppard," Ali said.

"Celeste Alexander," Celeste said.

Buster couldn't stop grinning. Jodi had hit the fucking jackpot! And by extension he had, too. This situation was going to present him with hours of serious high-quality fantasy entertainment. No doubt. He could picture it all. . . . His girlfriend and her two roommates getting dressed in the morning. His girlfriend and her two roommates getting undressed at night. His girlfriend and her two hot roommates accidentally walking in on each other in the shower. His girlfriend and her two hot roommates having a midnight, naked pillow fight—like in that movie from the seventies . . . *Animal Farm* or *Animal House* or whatever.

"Uh . . . whose idea was it to put all the beds together?" he asked. Suddenly the world seemed more wonderful than he had ever dreamed. Imagine all the girl triples in all the dorms in all the colleges in all the cities in all the countries! Imagine triples in Sweden and France!

"Nobody's," Jodi snapped. She stood up.

"We should do something about them," Celeste said.

THE ALPHABETICAL HOOKUP LIST

"Amen," Ali chimed in.

All three girls started frantically pulling the beds apart. The metal frames screeched loudly on the linoleum floor.

"Wait a minute!"

Celeste stiffened. *Jib?*

She whirled around and found herself staring at her parents, who were standing in the doorway. Her stomach contracted. What the hell were they doing back here?

"Before you rearrange the furniture, we should make sure the feng shui is right," Carla said. She strolled into the room, waving her arms dramatically. Her jewelry rattled. It sounded like wind chimes. "The desk by the door is blocking all the *qi*.[7]"

"Carla, what's going on?" Celeste hissed. She clenched her fists at her sides in a desperate effort to remain calm. "What are you doing back here?"

"We forgot to give you something," Jib said. He smiled at the other two girls. His eyes were red slits. "Aren't you going to introduce us?"

Celeste hung her head in misery. "Jodi Stein, Ali Sheppard, this is Carla and Jib," she said.

Jodi stared at them. "Are you our dorm advisers?"

"They're my parents," Celeste said quickly.

"What is feng shui?" Ali asked. She was curious. Celeste's parents sure as hell seemed a lot less uptight than Celeste. They also reeked of pot. *Good* pot.

□□□□□□□□□□□□□□□□□□□□□□□□□□□□

7 Pronounced "chee."

Carla smiled at Ali. "It's the ancient Chinese art of arranging furniture in order to allow the *qi,* or energy, to flow properly—therefore ensuring health, happiness, a sense of belonging, financial success, good grades, love, et cetera. For instance, it's very important to point your head in the right direction when you sleep."

Celeste rolled her eyes.

"So which way should my head point?" Ali asked.

"It depends what you're most interested in achieving," Carla said.

Ali smiled and closed her eyes. "A sense of belonging," she said dreamily.

"Then when you sleep, your head should point east."

Ali had no idea which way was east. *Hmmm.* The sun was almost setting, and the sun set in the west, so . . . *there.* She dragged the bed over to the east corner and placed it at an angle. Perfect. Now the "chee" would be all set.

Jodi hesitated a moment, then dragged her bed to another corner and tilted it at an easterly angle, too. Not that she was superstitious or anything. Celeste's parents were obviously freaks. But it couldn't hurt. And by the way, who referred to their parents by their first names, like they were coworkers or something?

"That looks ridiculous," Celeste said, making a mental note to move her bed to point east as soon as Jib and Carla left. "I'm putting my bed by the door."

"Oh, look at our baby, Jib," Carla said. "She has to be closest to the door. That's the true sign of a control freak and a Virgo—"

"So what did you forget to give me?" Celeste interrupted.

Jib and Carla gave each other a look. "Well, Celeste, college is a time for experimentation," Jib began.

Wherever this speech was going, Celeste was pretty much mortified that it was taking place in front of her new roommates, however awful they might be. And she had a pretty good idea where it *was* going, too. Jib was either going to give her one of his old bongs or pipes. Or something to put in it. . . .

"And we are all for experimenting," Carla said.

"We just want you to be safe. Safety first," Jib said.

"So we want to be the ones to give you this," Carla continued.

Jib reached into his jeans pocket and pulled out a large zip-locked bag of marijuana, which he handed to Celeste.

"Cool!" Buster said.

"You *guys.*" Celeste groaned, holding the baggie up between two fingers like some kind of criminal evidence. "You know I don't smoke."

"Well, maybe it's time to give it a try," Jib said in a gentle tone, as if he were a guidance counselor. "There's nothing wrong with getting high every once in a while, sweetheart."

So I can run around in a leopard-skin poncho and scream, "I am the Lizard King!" like you did two nights ago? Celeste wondered. Right. That was exactly the kind of college student she wanted to be. Good old Jib. He always came through with great advice at just the right time.

"Or even more than once in a while," Jib added. He

grinned stupidly at Carla and winked. They both laughed. He reached back into his pocket. "And here are some rolling papers."

"Wow, your parents give you all the best school supplies," Ali murmured.

"Remember, we're not encouraging you to do it," Carla said. "We want you to make your own decisions. But if you *do* decide to do it, we want you to get it from us so that we can be sure it's safe. And that goes for acid and X, too. *All* drugs."

Celeste tried not to groan. Jib and Carla had to be the only two parents on the entire planet who used "drugs" and "safe" in the same sentence.

Jodi, Ali, and Buster couldn't believe what they were hearing. This was so trippy. Literally.

"Wow," Buster said. "My parents just gave me one of those giant tins of three kinds of popcorn—cheddar, caramel, and plain—that you can use as a wastepaper basket when all the popcorn is finished. I can't imagine them giving me a giant tin of weed, ecstasy, and 'shrooms."

"Yeah, I doubt I'm going to be getting any care packages like that from home," Jodi said. Maybe Celeste wasn't going to be such a bad roomie after all.

"Anyway, we didn't mean to make such a big deal out of it," Jib said. "We should get going. But first I suggest we recite a Zen koan to sanctify your auras and living space."

Please, God . . . or Qi, or Krishna, or Buddha, or whoever, Celeste prayed, *deliver me from this nightmare.*

Jib opened the windows wide and took some sort of thick green herb stick out of his pocket. He struck a match under one end and held it there until the top was really smoking. In an instant everyone's face shriveled up like a raisin. It smelled vile—like burning, fetid cheese. Jib waved the stick all over the room, making crazy circles with it in the air and in every corner, over the beds and desks, and all over the three girls. Celeste shook her head at him. He looked like a little kid playing with a toy helicopter.

"This is a sage bundle, otherwise known as a smudge stick. We perform this smudging to clear the air of all past negative energy," he said.

What about present negative energy? Jodi thought—but she didn't say it out loud.

"Now, everyone stand in a circle and hold hands," Jib said.

Ali giggled. Jodi took a step back. Celeste squeezed her eyes shut. Was it too soon to transfer?

"Come on, guys, you're roommates now. You've got to break the ice," Carla said. She shuffled around the room, grabbing everyone and forcing them to stand in a circle and hold hands. She tried to prop Buster up against her because he was having trouble balancing on one leg, but he wriggled free of her grasp.

"Uh, I've got to get going," Buster said. "Jodi, I'll pick you up later for dinner. Bye." He ran out of there as fast as his two crutches could carry him.

Celeste mouthed a silent "sorry" to her new roommates. Ali didn't notice. She was too busy staring at Jib with an intense, wide-eyed expression—but Celeste couldn't tell if it was amusement or awe or fear, or some combination thereof. Jodi shrugged.

Celeste wanted to crawl under one of the beds and die. This was even more humiliating than when Jib had done this to Celeste's whole ninth-grade class on her first day of high school.

"Oh, Lord of Creation," Jib intoned, "please bless room 213 and let it be a place of truth and balance and growth and love and learning."

Ali started laughing. She couldn't help herself. And it was the really bad kind of laughing where you're trying to hide the fact that you're laughing by coughing. Then she just let loose. Jib stared at her. *Talk about a freak!* she thought. He was amazing. So was this woman in the muumuu, Carla. Why couldn't Ali's parents go by their first names? Celeste didn't know how lucky she was. Too bad *they* weren't moving in. Ali could almost see herself dealing with a triple if Celeste's parents were her roommates. Yeah, totally. She could become a hippie! That might actually be sort of cool: smoking weed, listening to the Grateful Dead (okay, maybe not *that*), cruising the open highway on a motorcycle. . . .

Jib looked hurt.

"Sorry," Ali choked out between laughs. "Really, it's just—"

"Well, that should do the trick," Carla stated. She shot Ali a cold glare, then looked adoringly at her husband. "That was lovely, Jib. Thank you so much for that."

"I'm just trying to get you girls started on the right foot," Jib said.

"I know, Jib, thanks," Celeste muttered. She didn't know what else to say. This was truly awful. A new parental low. She just wanted them to get lost as fast as possible—and for this Ali person to shut the hell up.

"I'll bring the rest of your things upstairs," Jib said. He left with Carla following him.

Ali finally managed to get a grip on herself. The triple was silent. The three girls stood there, looking at one another.

"So," Ali said. "Here we all are."

Then she started laughing again.

4

Go, go, go, PU!

Jodi was delirious. Now, *this* was what college was all about: lounging by a pool, watching water volleyball, and sipping a delicious rum-and-fruit cocktail called jingle juice. She was actually pretty fucked up. She closed her eyes and grinned up at the sun as her brand-new friends splashed all around her. She couldn't believe how fast she'd made friends. Or how easy it was to avoid the triple. Almost overnight she'd fallen in with a bunch of other girls in Maize Hall who were also Kappa Kappa Gamma pledges: Mandi, Buffi, Wendi, Hallie[8] . . . and also, unfortunately, Hallie's roommate: lazy-eyed, narcoleptic K. J. Martin.

But even *that* was okay. Because the best part was that Mandi's boyfriend, Ken, was a senior who lived off campus. He had his own studio apartment in a complex with a pool and a Jacuzzi and a gym. It was about as close to heaven as

[8] A British exchange student who had her own karaoke machine.

Jodi could ever imagine. It was almost enough to make her forget that her belongings still hadn't arrived.

Almost.

Jodi's smile faltered. Actually, in spite of her plastered state, she couldn't help but feel a little ill. Having two room-mates was one thing. Having no answering machine for their phone was another. *That* sucked. But having no clothes? Having no hair dryer? That was beyond sucking. Her only con-solation was that she owned a Volkswagen Beetle. She didn't get it, though. Nothing for Jodi Stein—or even Josi Stein— had ever showed up at the UPS office. Now, obviously no one was more excited about being at Pollard than she was. But she was getting a little tired of getting up every morning to buy a new PU sweat suit, new PU socks, and new PU boxer shorts. Last night she had written *learn how to do that whole laundry thing* in the things-to-do section of her Filofax.

She would have raided Buster's closet if he'd had any nor-mal clothes, but she really didn't relish wearing a T-shirt that said Take Me Drunk I'm Home or one that said Death Before Marriage, with a picture of a noose on it. (Of course, Buster could pull off wearing shirts like that because he was so dev-astatingly cute.) She also couldn't exactly borrow clothes from her darling roommates. From what she could tell, that Alison chick had absolutely no clothes that weren't (*a*) black, (*b*) Day-Glo, or (*c*) made of vinyl. And Celeste dressed like Madeline.[9] *Screw 'em.* At least Celeste had taken the liberty

---

9 Children's book character: little French schoolgirl who wears a blue coat and yel-low hat.

of plugging in a Glade vanilla air freshener to get rid of the smell of Jib's shit stick or sage stick or whatever it was—which would hopefully wipe the whole ugly memory from everyone's minds.

Yes, that was all in the past. Now everything was going according to plan. Just the way Jodi had always pictured it. She loved college. She loved everything about it. *Go, go, go, PU! Go, go, go PUKE. . . .*

Suddenly Jodi knew she was about to puke.

Maybe it was all the fruit in the jingle juice. She'd pretty much drained the punch bowl. Or maybe it was the rum. Or maybe it was the fact that in the past twenty-four hours, the only thing she'd eaten besides jingle juice fruit was a plate of onion rings. Whatever the reason, she was in big trouble. She was sitting at a deck table with this hideous, blond, fake-breasted, bitchy girl (the only lame Kappa Kappa Gamma pledge, as far as she could tell) who for some reason hadn't said one word to her . . . and besides, she was way too drunk to stand up and try to find a bathroom. And it was too late, anyway. She puked in her own hands.

"Eeew!" the bitchy girl shrieked. "Eeew! Jodi's throwing up in her hands."

"Grow up," Jodi moaned. She leaned over and rinsed her hands out in the dregs of the jingle juice.

"Eeew, eeew!" the girl kept screaming.

"Shuddup," Jodi slurred, trying to stand. "It's all done, anyway—"

"Eeew. That is so gross. Where did you learn manners like that? Is that what they taught you on Long Island?"

Jodi attempted to frown but ended up burping. "Who are you talking to?" she muttered. "Nobody is even listening to you."

"*Excuse* me," the girl snapped indignantly. "Everybody here is listening to me. For your information, my name is Augusta DuBois, and I—"

"Shuddup!" Jodi barked. In an attempt to both steady herself and wipe her fingers clean, she leaned forward and placed her pukey/juicy hands on Augusta DuBitch's head.

"No!" Augusta DuBitch screamed. She looked like she had bits of pink oatmeal in her hair.

Jodi smiled. The deck spun around her. Maybe she should leave now, before everybody started staring. Good idea. She grabbed a half-drunk beer off the table and rinsed off her hands with what was left in the can, then wandered out of the yard. It was time to hoof it back to campus. Her orientation group was having its tour of the school, and she didn't want to miss it. She wished she had driven. Where was a chauffeur when you needed one?

The freshman class was divided into groups of eight for the orientation tour. Jodi was the last to arrive for hers. The walk hadn't sobered her up, but she was still very relieved: neither Celeste Alexander nor Alison Sheppard was standing with the little posse in front of the library. Not that the assembled freaks were that much better. It looked like they were freshmen in high school as opposed to freshmen in college.

"Sorry I'm laid," Jodi slurred. She hiccuped and laughed. "I mean, late."

The most depressed-looking girl of the bunch stared at Jodi. Then she cleared her throat and turned her attention back to the others. "As I was saying, I'm Natalie. I'm an RA and your personal tour guide this evening." She was wearing a long black skirt and a black top and orange sneakers, which looked very strange. "I'd like to officially welcome you to PU."

"Cha," Jodi said.

Natalie looked at her again. "Yes?"

"It's cold in here," Jodi said, even though they were standing outside. She looked down at herself and noticed that her PU sweat suit had soaked through in the boob and crotch areas. Whoops. She'd forgotten to change out of her bathing suit before putting on her clothes. "I'm thirsty. Do you have any fruit?"

Natalie chose to ignore her. "This is the Allween Library," she said. "It's the biggest building on the PU campus. Please follow me."

Jodi staggered after the group. *Wow,* she thought. She felt as if she were standing at the bottom of a tornado. The library was huge and spinning when you were in the atrium. It was very dramatic. It was eight stories tall, and you could look up at the interior balconies of all eight floors towering above you. You could really start to feel queasy if you kept your eyes open—

"The Allween Library has a very rich history," Natalie announced. "There have been six suicides here since its official naming ceremony in 1853. In fact, there was one the week that it opened."

Jodi stared at her blankly.

"There was one additional incident in the eighties, around the time John Lennon was assassinated outside of his New York City apartment building, but nobody knows if it was a suicide or if in fact it was a murder. The case is still unsolved. The victim showed no typical signs of a suicide. She had not shown apparent signs of depression, had not sought counseling, had said nothing to friends, and hadn't left a note. She had, however, recently checked out a copy of *The Catcher in the Rye,* by J. D. Salinger."

"Cool," one kid said.

"Oh, I loved that book," Jodi said. "Holy Cornfield!"

"Holden Caulfield," Natalie corrected Jodi. Then she looked at her. "Do you realize that you stink of booze?"

Jodi shrugged. "Yeah, but what're you gonna do?"

A couple of kids moved away from her.

Natalie continued the tour. They went to the theater next. A girl had hanged herself in the costume department. After that, it was off to the science lab. Along the way Jodi learned how many suicides had taken place on campus since the school was founded, as well as how many deaths had occurred by choking, fire, drunk driving, overdoses, and aneurysms. Natalie had gone to the trouble of categorizing each suicide: most romantic, most gruesome, most easily preventable, most unusual circumstances, most legendary, most tragic. She also listed the probable causes: failing grades, psychosis, unrequited love, closeted homosexuality, unwanted pregnancies.

The tour ended in the stable. Jodi had never been in a real stable before. It stank.

"This is where the equestrian club meets," Natalie said.

"PU," Jodi said. She teetered in the straw.

"Yes? What about PU?" Natalie asked.

"PU—it stinks in here!" Jodi said. She grinned at the others, then burst out laughing.

Natalie's eyes narrowed. She turned her back on Jodi. "Anyway, one of the strangest deaths in the history of the university occurred here in these very stables. A graduate student, apparently writing her thesis on Queen Katherine the Great, tried to re-create the scene where Katherine has sex with a giant steed. This student attempted intercourse with PU's own horse Equinox, ostensibly for research purposes. The student died a horrible death and was carried out naked, covered only by a horse blanket, and brought to Athens General. George, the stable man, saw the whole thing. . . ."

Jodi stopped listening. She was realizing that she had a lot in common with a horse. She was about to fall asleep standing up.

". . . thanks very much for your time," Natalie concluded. She handed everyone a business card with her name and the number for PU's suicide hotline.

"Great!" Jodi said. "Thanks! I'll give you a call." She was about to put it in the business card networking section of her

Filofax when she remembered something: she had no idea where her Filofax was. And then she remembered something else. *Buster!* They'd agreed to meet as soon as their tours were over. What a relief. She'd finally be able to have a conversation with a normal human being.

"I'm so excited about rushing Kappa Kappa Gamma," Jodi told Buster over the third cup of coffee he had bought for her. He was trying to sober her up. It was so sweet. A first, too. Usually, given the opportunity, Buster always tried to ply her with booze. Maybe this was a sign: he was finally growing up. They were becoming adults together. It was so romantic. They sat in Blue Sky Coffee, the café right off campus, just like real grown-ups. Jodi had changed out of her wet clothes into new sweatpants and a T-shirt Buster had lent her. It was black, except for the word *pimp* printed in white letters. At least it was more understated than most of them.

"So what's your first rush activity?" Buster asked.

"An Alice in Gammaland party at the house," Jodi said. "We have to dress up as our favorite *Alice in Wonderland* character."

Buster smirked. "I heard that sororities torture the pledges, but I didn't know they went that far. That's cruel."

"Well, how about *you?*" Jodi asked, sipping her coffee.

"I'm not allowed to say."

Jodi frowned. "Come on. I just told you what *I* have to do."

"The guys at Beta Phi don't want me talking," Buster said.

"But Buster, come on," Jodi murmured. She reached

under the table and massaged his bulging thigh. "We share everything, remember?"

Buster shrugged.

Jodi's fingers inched closer to his crotch. She raised her eyebrows.

"Oh, all right." Buster glanced around the coffee shop, then leaned close to her and lowered his voice to a whisper. "But you have to swear you won't tell anyone."

"I swear," Jodi said.

Buster smiled. "We have to sit bare-assed on a block of ice for twenty minutes, doing beer bongs. Then we drink a beer, and they stick a golf ball in between our butt cheeks. Then we have to walk up a flight of stairs, chugging a beer the whole time. If the golf ball falls out, we have to shotgun a beer and do it all over again."

Jodi blinked. She could feel the coffee churning in her stomach. "You're joking, right?"

"Nope." Buster leaned back in his chair, a proud grin on his face.

"You're actually gonna let some guy stick a golf ball up your butt?"

"Shhh!" Buster hissed. He took another look around the coffee shop. "They're not gonna stick it *up* my butt," he whispered. "Just between the butt cheeks."

Jodi stared at him. "Oh," she said. She wasn't quite sure of the difference. "Well, isn't that . . . you know? Sort of gay?"

"Not half as gay as dressing up like a gay character from some gay children's book," Buster muttered.

"But . . . ," Jodi began, then decided against it. It was best not to pursue this topic of conversation. Not unless she wanted to puke again. No, it was best just to dwell on the positives. "You know, I really love it here, Buster."

"Me too," he said.

"PU is everything I hoped it would be. It's everything I imagined. Buster, I'm so happy. I love the people I've met—well, most of them. I love the campus. I love the bookstore. I love the sports center."

"Jo, I'm really proud of you," Buster said.

"Really?" Jodi asked, blushing slightly. "Why?"

"You've really kept up your tan since you've been here. You look awesome."

"Thanks," Jodi said, pleased.

He took her hand under the table. "I think we gotta get you home to bed."

By home, Buster meant his dorm, not hers—and by bed, Buster meant his as well. Jodi had spent every single night in Buster's room so far. She couldn't bear spending a night with Celeste and Alison in that triple.

"Let's stop by my place first and see if my stuff arrived yet," Jodi said.

Buster nodded. "Okay. I'll meet you at my dorm. I'm afraid of your room. That freak cursed it with his smelly stick."

"Tell me about it." She groaned.

"Hey, which reminds me: Ask that chick Celeste if we can borrow some of her weed," Buster said. "My bros in Beta Phi would be psyched on that."

5

Celeste couldn't wait for her orientation tour. She carefully selected an outfit in the dorm: black pants and a cream-colored sleeveless turtleneck sweater from J. Crew. It was sophisticated, yet fun. Exactly how she'd imagined looking in college. She grabbed her special orientation notebook and went to meet her group.

Orientation week. Sorority rush. The freshman play at the Bee. The Beer Blast in Stonewall Field. The Pub Crawl. Suicide Row at Allween Library. . . . The names and places and activities whirled through Celeste's mind as she dashed across campus. It was all so exciting.

She had prepared a list of questions to ask her orientation leader. For one thing, she wanted to know if she could declare a theology major with a minor in psychology right away—or if it was better to wait until the end of sophomore year. She also wanted to know how to get the second-semester reading lists now. And of course she was going to pull the leader aside and ask about the therapy that was available to students through the health clinic. She really wanted to get started discussing some of her issues with a psychologist (or at least a psychologist in training)—namely, her issue about why it was so hard for her to actually hook up with a guy. One of her big goals at college was falling in love. And *soon*.

She'd had boyfriends at Stuyvesant—her high school back in New York—but she hadn't gotten intimate with them. She had gotten pretty close with her boyfriend senior year, Edward. On their final date of the summer he had taken her to a trendy restaurant in Midtown called La Fundue, a place that had about twenty different kinds of fondue. They'd ordered strawberry daiquiris. Celeste had gotten a little more drunk than she had realized. She'd leaned forward to kiss him, and the next thing she knew, she'd singed her eyebrows in the gas flame under the fondue pot. She'd been forced to rush home, and Edward had sat with her while she put an ice compress on her forehead. Celeste had thought about doing it with him that night, but the accident had sort of killed the mood. To make matters worse, when he left, Jib and Carla had accused him of being gay. They were slumped over their Nepalese hookah pipe, screaming, "Our daughter the fag hag," and laughing hysterically.

Celeste did not appreciate her parents' sense of humor.

She wasn't really sure why she and Edward had never done it. She'd wanted to do it, but she just couldn't let it happen. She'd get nervous. Or his theater group would call an emergency rehearsal and their date would get canceled. So here she was at college, a coed, and a virgin at eighteen. And she knew she really couldn't blame it on Edward. She was obviously scared of intimacy.[10]

Maybe there would be a great guy in her orientation group. She was excited to meet other people. Of course, she had gotten off to a terrible start with her roommates, no thanks to her parents—but also no thanks to the fact that Jodi and Alison were shallow, vapid party girls.

Celeste's hopes sank a little when she saw the group assembled in the appointed meeting place outside of the dining hall. There were four boys and three other girls standing there, and all of them looked bored. . . . *But wait.*

Actually, one of the boys was nicely dressed and very cute. He was tall and slim, wearing khaki pants that hung just right on his hips and a billowy maroon shirt—whereas the other boys looked like they were dressed for the beach. Or worse. One of them had a mullet and was wearing a T-shirt with a Confederate flag on it. He looked as though he would be going right from the orientation tour to his Aryan Nation youth meeting. The nicely dressed boy was also the only boy not wearing a baseball cap. He had nice, soft-looking, straight black hair and blue eyes that reminded her of the water in Ibiza, an island she'd been to off the coast of Spain.

She and the nicely dressed boy were the only ones wearing their orientation name tags. His said *Jordan Cole.* She and

□□□□□□□□□□□□□□□□□□□□□□□□□□□□□□□

10 Everyone's scared sometimes.

Jordan were also the only two holding notebooks and pens. Didn't anyone else care about learning about their school?

He caught her eye and smiled at her.

"Hi," he said.

Her face turned red. She quickly looked down at her shoes. "Hi," she mumbled.

He walked over to her and peered at her name tag. "Celeste? That's pretty. When I was a little kid, I had an imaginary friend named Celeste."

"Really?" Celeste looked up. Having an imaginary friend was so adorable. "What did the two of you do?"

"Oh, gee. I don't know if I can tell you. That's pretty personal." Jordan smiled. "Me and old Celeste, we spent a lot of time together. We talked a lot and played pick-up sticks."

"Pick-up sticks!" Celeste said, completely delighted. This was such a strange conversation.

"I know," Jordan said. "It was pretty intense. Did you have an imaginary friend?"

"No," Celeste said. *Just imaginary parents,* she thought. "Has our leader showed up yet?" she asked, changing the subject.

"No," Jordan said.

"Yeah, he has," a boy said, jumping into their conversation.

"Where is he?" Celeste asked.

"In front of your face," the boy said. "I am your mighty leader!"

Celeste looked him up and down. How could this kid be an

RA? He looked like he was about seven. He was wearing shorts with holes in them and a baggy Hawaiian shirt.

"My name is Erik Shoenman," the RA said.

"Your parents named you Erection Man?" Aryan Nation Boy asked.

"It's Erik Shoenman," the RA said, enunciating clearly.

"Hey, Erection Man," the boy insisted.

"Ha ha. Very funny," Erection Man said. "Actually, I kind of like it. I've never thought of it that way before. I am Erection Man!" He stood straight, like a superhero. Then he put his hands on his hips and thrust out his crotch. "Hey, all you horny girls out there in Pollard City, fear not, for Erection Man is here. Erection Man to the rescue!"

Celeste gaped at him, horrified.

"You can put your notebook away," Erection Man said to Celeste. "Unless you want to write any of this down."

Everyone laughed, except for Celeste and Jordan.

"He looks more like Little Bulge than Erection Man," Jordan whispered in Celeste's ear.

Celeste let out a tiny chuckle. She actually felt a little sick.

Several people burst into song behind her. She turned around and found herself staring at a nerdy-looking quartet of boys, all of whom were wearing sweatshirts with the same logo, The Quarter Notes, in girlie script. They were singing the PU anthem in perfect a cappella harmony:

"Pollard University, the pride of Dixiela-a-and!

"Pollard University, the pride of—"

"Whoa, whoa, whoa, cut that shit out!" Erection Man snapped.

The quartet wandered off, still singing.

Erection Man shook his head in disgust. "This, ladies and gentlemen, is a PU orientation week tradition. Gay men wander the campus, singing. There is nothing you can do to stop it." He wagged a finger at the Quarter Notes. "This is why we are a drug nation."

"What do you mean, Erection Man?" one of the girls asked.

"Well." He paused and looked at the girl's name tag. She had neglected to write her name on it. "Well, No Name, I'm glad you asked. We are a drug nation because after a week of this, you will simply be *needing* to do a lot of drugs. For that, too, is a PU tradition. As is promising that they will provide the campus with answering machines, then failing to do so. But hey, at least we have phones."

Celeste and Jordan glanced at each other.

"And now for our tour," Erection Man said.

"Will we be touring the campus chapel?" Celeste asked hopefully.

"Why? Do you two want to get married?" Erection Man winked at both of them.

"No!" Celeste yelped. Her stomach plummeted. "I was just—you know, I was thinking about majoring in theology," she stammered. Her face turned bright red.

Jordan smiled. "Cool," he said. "Theology."

"Actually, there's only one stop on my tour," Erection Man said. "Please follow me."

The group followed Erection Man in silence, like children following the Pied Piper. Celeste didn't say a word. She was too embarrassed to speak. She simply walked next to Jordan, staring at the ground.

"Wandering the campus singing sounds like a lot more fun than following Mighty Prick, here," Jordan mumbled.

Celeste laughed.

Erection Man led them all the way to Hackman dorm. He didn't bother to point out any of the buildings or campus landmarks along the way. Around them, other happy tours were in progress; the informed RA leaders were walking backward and pointing to either side of them. In fact, the tour guides were known around campus by the name "Backward Walkers." With the exception of Erection Man, of course. Celeste thought seriously about just ditching him and joining one of the other groups. But something was keeping her there. And that something had a name.

Jordan.

Celeste could see herself really liking him. He was . . . what was the word she was looking for . . . *funny*. And nice. And very good looking, in that slim, male-model sort of way.

The group followed Erection Man into Hackman dorm and up to a large room with a bunk bed in one corner. The top bunk was unmade, and the bottom was unoccupied altogether: just a bare, thin, striped mattress. Posters covered every inch of the four walls. Most of them were of naked or partially dressed women, a few were of rock stars, and one was of different kinds of marijuana plants. There was a red lightbulb in the ceiling instead of a regular one.

"Roxanne," Aryan Nation Boy screeched. *"You don't have to put on the red light."*

"You don't have to put on the red light," all the others joined in, except for Celeste and Jordan. *"Put on the red light. Put on the red light. Put on the red light—"*

"Silence!" Erection Man barked. He smiled, then reached into a trunk at the foot of the bunk bed and pulled out a two-foot bong, a lighter, and a Jib-sized bag of pot. "All right. Everyone sit in a PU circle."

Celeste and Jordan looked at each other again.

Everyone else sat down in a circle. Erection Man lit the bong and began to pass it around to his left, starting with No Name.

Celeste started backing toward the door. All of a sudden she felt like crying. The smell of marijuana always reminded her of home. She wondered what Jib and Carla were doing.

"Uh, excuse me, but what are we doing after this?" Jordan demanded, standing at Celeste's side. He folded his arms across his chest.

"This is it," Erection Man said. "The tour ends here."

Jordan looked at Celeste. "Wanna split?" he asked.

"Yes," Celeste said automatically.

On their way out of the room they ran into a big fat woman—probably somebody's mother—sniffing the smoky air in the hall and shrieking to nobody in particular.

"I know I've died and gone straight to hell. I'll not have my child living in a crack den. You should all be ashamed of yourselves!" She locked eyes with Celeste. "What is a nice, pretty little girl like you doing in this place? What are you, then, one of those crack-head whores?"

Celeste's mouth fell open.

"We were just leaving," Jordan said. He took Celeste's arm and whisked her out of the dorm into the warm summer afternoon.

"Jesus," Celeste muttered, once she was able to catch her breath.

"I hope that woman isn't a professor here," Jordan said.

"I've never been called a crack-head whore before," Celeste said.

"It kind of suits you," Jordan said.

They looked at each other and started to laugh. They laughed for what seemed like a really long time.

"Where are you going now?" Jordan asked.

"I guess I'll go back to my dorm," Celeste said nervously. "I'm in Maize."

"Are you really thinking about majoring in theology?" Jordan asked.

"Definitely," Celeste said. She nodded, shoving the awful memory of Erection Man's room from her mind. "When your mother's an ex-nun and your father's an ex–Buddhist monk, you get kind of interested in the whole thing. They turned their backs on organized religion. Especially my mother. She ran away from the convent in the middle of the night and went straight to a commune. Studying theology is sort of my own way of rebelling, I guess."

"Wow," Jordan said, running his fingers through his gorgeous straight black hair. "What an amazing story. It's very *Sound of Music*. You know, I'm really interested in theology, too. I think it was Jean Paul Sartre who said, 'Without sinners there would be no need for priests.'"

Celeste's eyes widened. This was almost too perfect. "You read Sartre?" she breathed.

"Definitely—I love Sartre. You know, I read somewhere that they're actually showing *The Sound of Music* in movie theaters around the country, but it's called *Sing-Along Sound of Music*. They show the lyrics to all the songs on the bottom of the screen, and people in the audience go dressed up as characters in the movie. It's supposed to be hilarious. People really get into it. Hey, maybe you and I could go dressed as nuns. I'll try to find out when it's coming to the Atlanta area."

"Oh, um . . . tha-that would be great," Celeste stammered. Was he asking her out on a date? It was kind of a strange idea for a date. But it sounded like fun, and at least she wouldn't have to worry about what to wear since they would both apparently be dressed as nuns.

"Are you going to the Mint Julep Jamboree tomorrow night?" Jordan asked.

"I'm not sure," Celeste said. "I think so."

"Maybe we could go together," Jordan said.

"I . . . uh . . ." Celeste shrugged and grinned idiotically.

Jordan probably thought she had some sort of developmental delay. Which, in a way, she supposed she did. She was eighteen years old, and she'd never had sex.

Jordan flipped open his notebook and scribbled his phone number on a page, then tore it out and handed it to her. "Here," he said. "Give me a call, okay? Maybe we could even do something before then. You know, tonight. Just as a warm-up."

Celeste nodded. She couldn't even speak.

"Great. See ya." He walked away, and then he did *it.* The thing Celeste had hoped he would do. The thing that Oliver did to Jenny in the movie *Love Story* when he met her after his hockey game at Harvard. As Jordan was walking away he turned and smiled at her, walking backward a couple of steps, and then turned back around and continued on.

The tour might have started badly, but it had sure ended great.

6

Ali stood alone outside of Dimers, a pub on the edge of campus. She was supposed to meet her orientation group there, but no one had showed up. She looked at her watch—her grandfather's watch, the wearing of which was inspired by the short story "For Esme, With Love and Squalor," by J. D. Salinger, because Esme wore a man's watch.[11] It was almost nine o'clock. So Ali was on time. It felt sort of weird to start an orientation tour so late, but then again, what did she know? At least they were meeting at a bar, as opposed to the library or something. That was sort of cool.

She opened the door to the pub and looked inside, thinking maybe the group was in there. But there was just one dude sitting on a bar stool, talking to the bartender. He was dressed all in black. He looked Middle Eastern. There was no one else in the whole place.

"Can I help you?" the bartender asked.

---

11 Before she met Sensei, Ali went through a brief phase where she imitated characters from J. D. Salinger novels. It didn't get her very far.

"Uh . . . I'm supposed to meet some people," Ali said.

"For orientation?" the guy on the bar stool said.

"Yeah, uh, I guess," Ali said, feeling like a dork.

"Welcome! I'm your tour leader, Babak. And you are . . . ?" He took out an attendance list.

"Alison Sheppard."

"Great," he said, checking off her name. He patted the stool next to him. "Have a seat."

Alison shrugged and sat on the stool. The bar was hot. Her feet were sweating in her Doc Martens and black tights. She was wearing a ripped and safety-pinned T-shirt that said Look at Me Now. Dream about Me Later." Sensei had given it to her as a parting gift. The bar stools were the old-fashioned kind that were nailed to the floor and spun around. Ali resisted the urge to spin around like a little girl. She was a college student now. The only spinning she should be doing was behind the turntables. Not that she actually knew how to DJ. She left that to Sensei.

"So we'll start the tour," Babak said. "This is Dimers. It's one of the most important things for a freshman to know about because they serve mugs of beer for a dime."

"What kind of beer costs a dime?" Ali asked.

"Well, that's the thing," Babak said. "It's the sludge that was at the bottom of the kegs that were used at the sorority and fraternity parties on campus. But usually people come to Dimers after they've already been somewhere else, so they're already too drunk to know the difference."

"I see," Ali said. She couldn't tell if he was joking or not.

"Anyway, Dimers is the first place I ever got laid in a ladies' room," Babak said. "Her name was Angela."

Ali laughed. "Oh, yeah? Was it Angela Lansbury?"[12]

"Huh?"

Ali stared at him. He was sort of cute, in a dark and exotic kind of way—but he was clearly high on himself and not terribly bright. "You know, dude, I know this girl named Celeste. I could set you up with her, and then you could be Babak and Celeste."

"So? Yeah? Huh? I don't get it. Is she hot?"

"You know, like Ba*bar* and Celeste," Ali said. "King and queen of the elephants."

Babak smiled. "So far I haven't understood one thing you've said. But I like you."

Ali tried to smile back. The bartender placed a mug of sludge in front of her. She drank it. Then she drank another. Babak rambled on and on about all the hot freshman chicks he'd met this week. Ali kept stealing glances at her grandfather's watch. A half hour went by and no one else showed up. Ali was the only one. How hideous to be the only loser who showed up for orientation tour! *Damn.* Sometimes Ali felt like her whole life was the wrong end of a practical joke, and now was one of those times. In spite of the two-beer buzz, she was suddenly overcome with a feeling of incredible loneliness. It clutched at her stomach. She was completely isolated at this stupid college. Nobody else had showed up for the tour

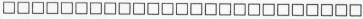

12 Star of *Murder, She Wrote.*

because they'd already all found scenes. Not her, though. Not only had she not made any friends yet, but she hadn't even seen any sign of her own roommates—whom she already knew she wouldn't like.

She wished she had gone to NYU with Sensei. She'd wanted to go to NYU. Unfortunately, NYU had rejected her. So had every other college except for PU. But that didn't matter—at least not in terms of the relationship department—because Sensei had solemnly sworn that he would be there for her no matter what. *"Even if I went to school in Hong Kong, in Bosnia, or on the moon, our relationship is too deep for distance, girl. Distance is in the mind. Our thing is in the soul."* Ali shuddered just thinking about it. He had such a way with words.

". . . then there was this chick Denise," Babak was saying. "Now, she was a real freak—"

"Would you mind if I made a quick phone call?" Ali interrupted.

Babak shrugged. "You're the only one who showed up. I can't be too picky about what you do. Beggars can't be choosers."

"Thanks," Ali mumbled.

She hurried outside and pulled out her cell phone. At least she had Sensei in spirit and voice, even if he wasn't there with her. She hit his name on autodial and listened to the phone ring. No way would he answer. Knowing Sensei, he'd probably already made two hundred great new friends and was opening his own club and becoming the new king of downtown New York.

"Hello?"

It was a miracle! Ali beamed. "Hey, it's me!" she exclaimed.

"Hrmm." It sounded like he had shoved something in his mouth. "What's up, girl? Don't mind me, I'm eating a falafel. They're only a buck seventy-five here. Man, they're so good. So what's the dilly-o?"

"The what?"

"What's the deal, girl? What's shaking?"

"Uh, not a whole lot, actually," Ali muttered. "You won't believe it. I'm stuck with this lame guy at what was supposed to be our orientation—"

"Hey, babe, I'd love to talk, but I can't right now. I'm going to a party. This dude I know is PJ."

"Who?" Ali's eyes narrowed. She didn't know anyone named PJ.

"The DJ!" Sensei swallowed loudly. "He's spinning. He's the DJ."

"Oh." Ali's heart sank. "You can't talk for just a second?"

Sensei said something, but Ali couldn't understand him. She just listened to him chew falafel. He sounded so far away, as if he really *were* in Bosnia or on the moon. Then again, that might be because her cheap-ass phone was made by the Megavox company.

"Hello?" Ali said. "Hello? Listen, Sensei, it's important to leave messages on my cell because we don't have an answering machine—"

"Bye." *Click.*

Ali's shoulders sagged. She went back into the bar.

Babak had switched from beer to Long Island iced tea.[13]

"Hey, dude, are there any raves around campus you could tell me about?" she asked. She wasn't going to feel sorry for herself. If Sensei could find a scene so fast, then she could, too.

"I know everything," Babak said. "That's why I'm your leader."

"Well?"

"Well, there's one tonight at a club called the 'Vous. That's short for Rendezvous, you know? It goes all night. Bring your spikes."

"My spikes?" Ali asked, confused.

"Anything spiked," Babak said. "Hair, heels, nipple rings, whatever you've got. Anyway, we might as well get started on the tour." He hopped off his stool and pointed at the bartender. "You the man, Tom."

The bartender ignored him.

Ali followed sulkily along after Babak. This was stupid. She had a rave to get to.

"So over there," Babak said, pointing to a garbage Dumpster next to a building. "That is where I had sex with Laura Norton."

Ali couldn't help but laugh. "You had sex in a garbage Dumpster?"

"No, not in it, freaky girl. Behind it. We did it *behind* the Dumpster."

They walked for a while in silence.

□□□□□□□□□□□□□□□□□□□□□□□□□□□□□□

13 Equal parts rum, tequila, vodka, gin, and triple sec, a splash of Coke, and a splash of sour mix.

"And over there, three floors up and the third window to the right," Babak said. "That's where Evelyn Robbins gave me a blow job. Man, was that good."

Ali frowned at him. Was he mistakenly laboring under the incredible delusion that anyone actually cared where he'd had sex?

"Now we are approaching Johnson Hall," Babak said. "It was here in Johnson that I had sex for the first time in one of those genuine ki*nippy* beds."

"What's a genuine ki*nippy* bed?" Ali asked.

"You know, all fluffy and ruffly with the part that hangs over your head. They have them in old, quaint hotels."

Ali laughed again. Truly Babak was an idiot. She only hoped that the rest of the guys at PU weren't as moronic. "Do you by any chance mean a canopy bed?" she asked.

"Yeah, whatever. Canopy, kinippy, who cares? The point is, I had sex in it," Babak said.

"Wait a minute," Ali said. "Is this the whole tour?"

"Of course not," Babak said. "I'm going to show you the shower where I accidentally walked in on Lisa Vincent."

"So this is, like, the Babak sex tour," Ali said.

"Well, don't look so disappointed," Babak said. "What were you hoping for, a tour of Hollywood stars' homes?"

"Yeah, okay, so this is where I get off the bus. Thank you. It was truly fascinating."

Babak shrugged. "Your loss. I was just going to take you over to Maize Hall. A lot of unbelievable shit happened to me there. I banged two freshmen at once last year. . . ."

Ali didn't hear the rest of it. She broke into a sprint, running away from Babak as fast as she could. No way would she let Babak's sex tour taint her own dorm. She glanced at her watch again. It was nine-forty. There was some sort of freshman dance at Grange Hall, but she'd pretty much had it with orientation activities. If she went, she'd probably be the only one there. Besides, she sort of felt like taking a nap before the rave.

Hopefully she'd have the place to herself.

No such luck.

When Ali arrived at room 213, her fellow triplets were there. It was only the third time they'd been together in the room since Celeste's father had blessed them or smudged them or whatever it was he had done. In fact, they had barely said two words to one another since they'd met, except concerning topics that were absolutely essential—like toilet paper (e.g., did they have to buy their own?).

There was an awkward silence as they all made note of this fact, followed by what could be called, at best, a stilted conversation.

"Hello," Celeste said.

"Hello," Jodi said.

"Hey, y'all," Ali said.

Jodi frowned.

Ali sniffed the air. "That stink is gone," she said.

No one replied.

"Well, I'm going to take a nap," Ali announced. She lay

down on her bed and turned on her side so she was facing the wall.

"I'm just checking to see if my stuff got here," Jodi said. "Then I'm going to Buster's." She was sort of talking to the air since nobody was really paying attention.

"I have a date," Celeste offered. Actually, she hoped they wouldn't be there when Jordan came to pick her up. On the other hand, she was pretty proud of herself.

"Really?" Jodi said. Talking about a date was interesting, even if the dater and datee were both total boobs. In fact, Jodi had always had a fascination with all kinds of couples— like when Siamese twins got married, or when midgets in the circus hooked up, or basically anything on *Jerry Springer* or *Howard Stern*. Deep down, she was a romantic. Because the most important thing she'd learned over the years was that no matter what kind of a freak you were, you had an ideal mate out there, somewhere in the world. Everybody belonged with somebody. Luckily *she'd* found her ideal mate in high school. But maybe Celeste would get lucky tonight. Jodi almost laughed out loud, thinking of Celeste on the *Howard Stern* show.

There was a polite but firm knock on the door. Celeste froze.

"You wait right there," Jodi told Celeste. "I'll get the door."

"Wait!" Celeste said, completely panicked. She ran to her bed and grabbed an armful of all the different outfits she had tried on for the date and shoved them in her little closet.

Jodi opened the door. A tall, cute, but somewhat geeky-looking guy with black hair was standing there. He was wearing a blazer with a name tag: *Hello, my name is . . . Jordan.*

"Hey," Jordan said.

"Hey," Jodi said.

"Hi, Jordan," Celeste said, stepping quickly toward the door. "I'm all ready, so we can just go."

Ali also couldn't resist sneaking a peek at Celeste's date. She turned over as nonchalantly as possible.

"This is a nice room," Jordan said. "But if I were you girls, I'd definitely paint it a color, maybe a deep blue."

Paint our room? Ali and Jodi both wondered at the same time.

"So let's go," Celeste said, maybe a little too eagerly. She didn't want to expose Jordan to her dumb roommates any longer than necessary. They might turn him off.

"Great!" Jordan said. "If you don't mind, I thought maybe I'd make you a little dinner at my place. I bought a recipe book called *Hot Plate Heaven,* and there's a delicious Hungarian goulash. And I purchased an Easy Bake oven so we can have some angel food cake for dessert. I think I'll eventually be able to figure out how to make a soufflé in it." He winked at her. "Just kidding. But it's the perfect touch of camp for a dorm made out of entirely synthetic materials, don't you think? All I need now is Tang mix."

Jodi grinned at Ali. FI: *Gay much?*

Celeste burst out laughing. "I *love* Tang," she said.

"Who doesn't?" Jordan asked.

Celeste grabbed her bag and her vintage beaded cardigan,

purchased at Alice Underground in New York, then hurried out the door.

Ali turned back around and faced the wall. Poor Celeste. The girl had a lot of learning to do. Clearly this Jordan character was as gay as the day was long.

A few minutes later Jodi left to meet Buster at his room in Hackman Hall.

"Bye, Ali," she said.

"Bye, Jodi."

Something occurred to Ali at that moment. "Bye, Ali" was the first normal thing Jodi had said to her since school had started. And that was a serious, serious bummer.

7

Jodi nestled deeper into Buster's underarm. She was getting used to sleeping in a single bed. It was so cozy always being this close to Buster, even if his cast made sleeping more difficult. (Not that they ever did a whole lot of sleeping, of course.) They'd placed a chair next to the bed so Buster could prop his leg up on it. He was a little too tall for the bed. His good foot hung out at the bottom. It was so cute.

In spite of her massive hangover, Jodi crawled on top of Buster and started kissing his neck. If she had to pick her absolute favorite part of college, it would be this: morning sex. It was the best. And it was something she and Buster had *never* had back at home on Long Island.[14] Morning sex was what it meant to be an adult.

Jodi thought back to her bat mitzvah speech about how she was an adult now, a woman, and what that meant to her. She wondered what her mother and father and Nana and

14 They'd had car sex, school sex, prom sex, parents' bed sex, and party sex.

Rabbi Abrams would have thought if she had said, "*Shem'a* Israel. Being an adult member of my community means getting laid in the morning."

Why am I thinking about Nana and Rabbi Abrams right now? Jodi asked herself with concerned surprise. She tried to wipe from her mind the image of her nana in her purple polka-dotted outfit, dancing freestyle to "Gangsta's Paradise."

"Stop it! Stop it at once!"

Jodi gasped. She rolled off Buster, only to find herself staring up at Nanjeeb, Buster's roommate. Nanjeeb was a native of Calcutta, India, and spoke with an English accent. He was wearing a bathrobe emblazoned with the Playboy bunny.

"That is enough, horny girl," Nanjeeb stated.

"Yo, homeboy," Buster muttered. He made no effort to pull the blanket over his boxer shorts, even though it was clear that Jodi had aroused him. "Do you mind?"

Nanjeeb's face twisted in a scowl. "Do I mind? Do I mind?" He thrust a finger at Jodi. "This is supposed to be a college dorm, not a bordello. Get out!"

Jodi's face turned bright red. Usually Nanjeeb was so quiet. Truth be told, she hardly ever realized that he was there. She could feel the remnants of the jingle juice stirring in her stomach. She started to crawl out of the bed, but Buster grabbed her arm.

"Just give us a minute, Nanjeeb, bro," Buster said.

"I certainly will not," Nanjeeb snapped. "This is not the best little whorehouse in Georgia. I can't stand this anymore.

'll just have to find someplace else to have sex with your
spoiled little tramp."

Jodi frowned. Suddenly she wasn't embarrassed anymore.
Suddenly she was just pissed. "Spoiled little *what?*" she
demanded.

Buster laughed. "All right. All right, bro. Just chill. We'll go
to the broom closet."

Jodi couldn't believe what she was hearing. "That's it?"
she asked Buster.

"What?" Buster said. "I thought you liked the broom
closet."

"You're just going to let him get away with calling me a
spoiled little tramp? Who *is* Nanjeeb, anyway? Your . . . your . . .
your *nana?*"

Buster seemed confused. "My nana?"

"Don't you dare call me Nana," Nanjeeb hissed. "Only my
mother and my aunt Tuli call me Nana. Just put your clothes
on and go."

"Fine," Jodi spat. She shook herself free of Buster's
grasp, then wriggled into her PU sweat suit and stomped
out of the room. She had better things to do than stick
around Buster's stupid dorm room, anyway. She had her
goddamn belongings to track down. They *still* hadn't
arrived. Every fucking morning at the Pollard mail room it
was the same old story: "No word as of yet, ma'am." And
who in God's name called an eighteen-year-old girl *ma'am?*
It was so—

"Wait! Jo!" Buster hobbled after her and stopped her in

the hall. "Hey, I'm sorry about that. But you know, we have to be careful."

Jodi shot Buster an icy glare. "You act like you're scared of him," she said.

"I *am* scared of him," Buster said. "He told me he has a head injury. I don't know what that means. I think he's crazy. You don't mess with a guy with a head injury."

"Whatever."

Jodi hurried out of the dorm. She knew Buster wouldn't be able to chase after her on his crutches. She stalked around campus for a while, too angry to do anything else. It was too early to go to the bookstore and buy something clean to wear; during orientation week the bookstore didn't open until noon. At least she had her car, she supposed. But there was nowhere to drive in it, except aimlessly around by herself. She had no idea where to find a Bloomingdale's or Macy's or *anything*—and besides, shopping for real clothes was only fun or worthwhile if you went with friends. She didn't know what to do. She was suddenly so lonely.

Daddy. Yes. Jodi would call her father. That's what she needed: a nice, long chat with Daddy to start the day right. Maybe she could even cash in on that big surprise he'd mentioned. If there were ever a time she needed a big surprise, it was now. She knew that at this moment he was sitting at his desk in his study, with a hot cup of coffee in front of him and maybe a piece of chocolate cake. He loved to take his breakfast in his study instead of in the kitchen, and he loved cake for breakfast more than anything. Except for his Jodi, of course.

found a pay phone right outside Maize and dialed her private number, using the special "Daddy Hot Line" ᴏne card he had given her.

"Hello?" he answered. His voice sounded gruff. He always sounded gruff in the morning.

"Daddy!" she exclaimed.

He cleared his throat. "Jo? That you? Is something wrong?"

Jodi swallowed. "No. Well, not really. I was just wondering, though. Remember that surprise you mentioned?"

"Yes?"

"Could I have it now? I've had sort of a rough morning."

Her father didn't say anything.

"Daddy?"

"Well, all right," her father said. His tone brightened. "I'd wanted to save it for a little bit longer, but what the hey! It sounds like my little girl could use some cheering up. You know I had a job working at a sardine cannery when I was in college, right?"

Jodi's eyes narrowed. "Um, yeah?" She wasn't following.

"It was a dangerous job," he said. "I almost lost a finger. But it was an *adventure,* Jo. It was *exciting.* It turned me into a man. More to the point, it taught me a lot about responsibility. It taught me about savings, about managing my own income, budgets, that sort of thing—"

"Daddy?" Jodi interrupted. "What are you talking about?"

He took a deep breath. "Well, your mother and I both agreed we should maybe stop spoiling you so much. No, *spoiling* isn't the right word. It's more that we don't want to keep you on a leash anymore. We've provided you with all sorts of amenities—your brand-new car, for example. The point is, it's time you started experiencing some adventure and responsibility yourself. It's time you started to learn what it's like to be an adult."

Morning sex, Jodi thought automatically. But she was on the phone with her father, so the thought kind of grossed her out. She shoved it from her mind.

"We're cutting off your allowance, honey," he said.

Jodi clutched the phone. Her pulse quickened. "Excuse me?"

Her father laughed, as if she'd just made a joke. "Look, Jo, it's liberating. Trust me. You'll thank me. Spending money you earned yourself on hair products or whatever else is so much more rewarding than . . ."

He went on and on while Jodi's mind raced. Adventure? Responsibility? What the hell was he talking about? Why were they doing this to her? This was not part of the plan. No way. What kind of job was she supposed to get, anyway? Tomorrow was the first day of classes. All the good jobs[15] were probably taken. This was so not fair. How were she and Buster supposed to fully immerse themselves in the PU social scene if she was *working?* This was a total nightmare. She didn't even have any clothes! How was she supposed to get a job in a sweat suit?

". . . sure you'll do just fine, honey. Now I—"

15 "Good jobs" is an oxymoron.

Beep beep beep. Symbolically, the "Daddy Hot Line" phone card ran out of money, and the line went dead.

Ali had finally found her scene.

Babak might be a testosterone-fueled jackass, but he did know where to find a good rave. And as Ali well knew, ravers were always the most accepting people, no matter where in the world you were.

At the 'Vous the night before, Ali had plunged headfirst into the pulsating beat and strobe lights and had been welcomed with open arms. These arms were a little different than the ones back home in Atlanta, though. As it turned out, everybody at this rave was antidrug and devoutly Christian. They were all wearing crucifixes and T-shirts that said things like: Meet Jesus! No Appointment Necessary. The only music they played was deep house, because there were no suggestive lyrics. It was extremely refreshing, although somewhat confusing—and deeply spiritual, what with twirling and waving glow sticks all night while alternately trying to read whatever she could of a pocket Bible that someone had slipped her in the dim light of the coed bathroom.

She had used squares of toilet paper as bookmarks for some of the harder passages so she could reread them when she wasn't so tired. There was a raver Bible study meeting today, and she was expected to read some whole chapter or other: Genesis, maybe. Unfortunately, the Bible was really no page-turner. Were there Cliffs Notes for the Bible? Monarch Notes? Anything?

She tried calling Sensei to see if he'd had any similar experiences with his rave friends in New York, but once again there was too much static. After "hello," she could only make out every second or third word of what he was saying, which was actually pretty funny. It sounded something like this: "I . . . fuck . . . to . . . ing . . . say . . . bush . . . you . . . blossom . . . like . . . what . . . falafel . . . go . . ." Maybe she could turn it into a spoken-word poem and enter a slam with it.

Ali looked at her watch and decided to blow off early morning group prayer at Blue Sky Coffee so she could catch up on some Bible reading before the meeting later. It was so exciting. This was really her thing. She was sure of it. And yes, Ali had tried a few things in her day. Okay, a lot of things. A couple of years ago she'd even tried that Madonna-inspired English accent.[16] But now she had really found something she could stick with. This was really *her.* She totally loved this whole thing. She just wished there was a little more *raving* involved and a little less *reading*.

Jodi shambled miserably into the triple—only to find Ali lying on her bed, reading the Bible, and Celeste standing at her desk, carefully wrapping a present for someone. It was some kind of tube-shaped object, a tin of something. She shook her head. Her two freakish roomies were getting freakier by the second. Today was shaping up to be a major

---

16 Although she'd actually sounded more like Dick Van Dyke in *Mary Poppins.*

suck fest. Why couldn't she have gotten a single? Why? Maybe she could start sleeping in her car.

"What's that?" she asked Celeste.

Celeste had that very specific, unmistakable look on her face that people only get if they're in love with somebody and that somebody is always filling up their mind, no matter what they're doing or saying.

"It's a present for Jordan," Celeste said.

"A present?" Jodi asked. "You shouldn't be giving him a present after one date. He should be giving *you* a present. What is it?"

"Nothing," Celeste mumbled.

"Come on, it has to be something," Jodi pressed. *Like maybe a* Wizard of Oz *action figure,* she added silently.

"Y'all, do you mind? I'm trying to study," Ali piped in.

"Let's see, what comes in a tube like that?" Jodi asked. "The only thing I can think of is a vibrator. You didn't get him a vibrator, did you?"

"That's so disgusting," Celeste said. "If you must know, it's pick-up sticks. It's a private joke between us. See, last night . . ." She didn't finish. She wasn't about to tell Jodi that she and Jordan had spent all last night attempting to make angel food cake (which they'd burnt every time, to much hysterical laughter) in Jordan's Easy Bake oven and how pick-up sticks was the game Jordan used to play with his imaginary friend Celeste. It was none of Jodi's business, anyway.

"Pick-up sticks?" Jodi said. "You've actually rendered me speechless."

Celeste ignored Jodi. She concentrated on wrapping. She could tell Jordan was the type of guy who cared as much about the thoughtful way a present was wrapped as the present itself.

"Pick-up sticks?" Jodi repeated, in a voice filled with disdain.

"Why are you in such a bad mood?" Ali asked her.

"Oh, no reason," Jodi muttered. She flopped down on her own bed. No, there was no reason at all for her to be upset—unless you considered that on top of everything else that had happened this morning, she had gone to the student employment bulletin board (where only the poorest and most pitiful students had to go) . . . and instead of finding a whole host of exciting employment opportunities, she'd just found one lone index card pinned to the board. Actually it hadn't even been pinned to the bulletin board; someone had stuck it on with a chewed piece of gum. And on that index card was the worst job she could ever have imagined: Dining Hall Duty—the night shift. *Why? Why? Why?* she had asked herself. Couldn't there be anything else? Even Sardine Cannery would have been better. It really would have.

So tonight, instead of going to the Alice in Gammaland party, she would be hanging out at the dining hall with a bunch of pathetic losers, cleaning the disgusting remnants of institutional food off cheap ceramic plates.

Hideouser and hideouser, to quote Alice herself.[17]

There was a knock on their door.

17 The real quote is, "Curiouser and curiouser."

"Who is it?" Jodi said.

"UPS," a man's voice said.

Okay, finally, one good thing, Jodi thought. Her stuff had arrived at last. She ran to the door and opened it.

Ali glanced up from her Bible. The dude was gorgeous in his brown UPS uniform. It was a fact of life: All UPS men were gorgeous. Ali could never figure out why.

"Jodi Stein?" the man asked.

"Yes," Jodi said.

"Here's your package." The man handed her one flat, square box wrapped in brown paper. He shoved his clipboard at her to sign. The name *Damien* was embroidered onto the pocket of his uniform.

"What is this?" Jodi asked.

"Who do I look like, Psychic Sylvia Brown? I just deliver 'em," the guy said.

"But where's the rest of my stuff?" Jodi wailed. "All my boxes? My clothes, my track trophies?"

Celeste snickered to herself. She noticed Jodi hadn't mentioned books.

Jodi signed for her package and closed the door, sadly holding the box in her hands. For a second she felt like she might cry. But she would never cry in front of her roommates.

"You sure packed light for college," Ali said, glad of an excuse not to read psalm three million and seven.

"Very funny," Jodi grumbled. She sat back down on her bed and unwrapped the box. Her eyes widened in disbelief. It was a deluxe Scrabble set. There was also a note, written in red pen and barely legible: *Here is your off-to-college present and a little spending money! Love, Nana.* Jodi looked at the spending money. It was an old, faded, wrinkly five-dollar bill. Her grandmother had probably washed it so it wouldn't be covered in germs. Jodi's jaw tightened. Scrabble? *Scrabble?* Her nana obviously didn't know a thing about college. Unless Scrabble was a new kind of upper, it really wasn't the kind of thing college students were into doing. But hey, the fiver would come in handy. Right now it was the only money she had.

Jodi stood and stomped over to her empty closet. She opened the door and tossed the Scrabble board inside—then slammed the closet shut. Celeste flinched.

"See you guys later," Celeste mumbled. She hurried out of the triple with her perfectly wrapped present.

Jodi sat back down on her bed.

"Did you hear something when you opened the closet just now?" Ali asked.

"Like what?" Jodi snapped.

"Like Jordan? I was sure I heard him in there, screaming to come out."

Jodi stared at Ali. A little grin crept across her face.

The next thing she knew, both she and Ali were laughing hysterically.

It still sucked to have roommates, of course. But if Ali could make Jodi laugh on what was becoming the worst day of her life, she had to be good for *something*.

8

So this was what it meant to have a job. To be an "adult." The night before classes, while almost every single freshman was partying on frat row or at the bars that served minors, Jodi was up to her elbows in Chinese food,[18] with hot steam gusting up into her face and frizzing her hair. It was so horrible. Her father might have almost lost a finger at his first real job, but this was far worse. Even at a sardine cannery, there was no way her father had ever had to deal with anything that could destroy a girl's hair.

To make matters even more hideous, Buster hadn't come to visit her once during the whole shift. Not even to say hi. He was out with the normal people, having fun without her. Her coworkers, as it turned out, were anything *but* normal. In fact, most were ex-convicts. No joke. They were participating in a diversity program that allowed them to attend some classes for credit in exchange for doing work on campus. And they were the best of the bunch.

18 A euphemism for noodles smothered with some sort of grayish meat-and-sauce product.

The worst one was a junior named Zack. She'd heard people described as "wild haired" before, but she had never met anyone who fit the description better. Zack's hair was like an Afro—only light brown. It was as big and round and fuzzy as Bob Dylan's hair on the cover of *Blonde on Blonde.* Come to think of it, Zack looked as though he were trying to copy everything about Bob Dylan circa 1966, right down to his mysterious little half-smile and his heavily lidded brown eyes. It was so lame. He wasn't doing any work, either. Instead of cleaning the dumpling tray, with all the little asses of the dumplings still stuck to it, he was taking his tenth break and smoking these stinky little brown cigarillos. She didn't know which smelled worse, Zack's cigarillos or the food. No—what was worse was that he insisted on smoking them *in* the kitchen while *she* was trying to work. It was beyond rude. It wasn't even allowed.

She really felt like she was going to throw up.

"Zack, do you mind not smoking those in my face?" Jodi finally demanded.

Zack exhaled a big, toxic cloud. "Can you believe they have the nerve to charge so much for tuition—and this is the crap they serve? They pay us so little and we work so hard."

"We?" Jodi muttered. Actually, he was less like a young Bob Dylan and more like Pigpen from *Peanuts.* "If you don't like it, why don't you quit? Or better yet, transfer?"

"I only took this job to sow the seeds of revolution in the proletariat," Zack said.

Jodi grunted. "Ugh."

"I like your T-shirt," Zack said. "It's really quite profound."

Jodi was wearing one of Buster's favorites: Homer Simpson lying on a couch, holding a beer, with the words Living La Vida Sofa.

"What's your major?" Zack asked her.

"Training animals for the circus—elephants, mostly," Jodi said. She grabbed another tray off the cart and started scrubbing it.

"I'm in the noblest major," Zack said.

Jodi rolled her eyes. Who the hell had ever heard of a "noble" major?

"Philosophy," he offered, when she didn't ask.

"Figures," Jodi said, shoving an industrial-sized sponge into his hand. "Here, you finish sowing your seeds—I've *got* to get out of here."

It was only eleven. There was still time to have fun. She didn't think she'd be able to make it to Alice in Gammaland (after all, she had nothing to wear), but at least she could hang with Buster. He was probably still at Beta Phi Epsilon. He was *always* at Beta Phi Epsilon. They had already given him a bid, and bids weren't usually handed out until the end of the first semester. He was already tight with all the brothers, his new best friends. They had even asked him to be in their whiffle ball league. It was so unfair. Jodi had hardly been able to rush Kappa Kappa Gamma at all yet.

As soon as Jodi arrived at the frat house, she regretted not having gone back to the triple to borrow some clothes.

Between her two roommates there had to be *some* way she could have scrounged together a decent and sexy outfit. Even Celeste's plaid skirt and Monica Lewinsky's beret would have been better than Homer Simpson.

"Hi, have you seen Buster?" she asked a few guys. But no one paid any attention to her. She caught a glimpse of herself in the cracked mirror over the fireplace,[19] and to her horror, she looked as wild-haired as Zack. She made a note to herself to get to work early next time so she could work the salad bar instead of the steam trays.

Well, one thing was certain: She had to try to fix herself up before she ran into Buster. Unfortunately, the line for the ground-floor bathroom spilled out into the living room.

"Come on, I gotta go!" one guy yelled, banging on the door. "Next time try Metamucil!"

To Jodi's horror, he grabbed a ramen Cup O' Noodles[20] off the floor, peeled the lid off the styrofoam cup, unzipped his pants, and pissed into the cup until the noodles and tiny carrot squares were overflowing onto the floor. Maybe half a dozen guys were watching. Nobody said a word.

"What are you *doing?*" Jodi shrieked.

He didn't answer. He simply placed the Cup O' Pee on a side table and disappeared back into the party. A moment later an unknowing freshman geek—at least Jodi assumed he was a freshman because he had Coke-bottle glasses and

19 The only un-beer-stained surface in the entire house.

20 Fattening.

looked to be about twelve—picked up the cup and eyed it hungrily.

"Do you know where I can find a spoon?" he asked.

Jodi clamped her hands over her mouth.

A few kids laughed.

"Try the kitchen," someone said to him. "Although maybe you'd prefer split *pee*."

The kid didn't get it. He brought the soup to his nose and took a big whiff. Slowly it registered on his face that something might be wrong. "Hey, does anyone know if this stuff has an expiration date?" he asked.

"No, that stuff never goes bad," another guy said to him.

Gross. Jodi couldn't stand there and watch this. Forget it; she didn't care *how* she looked. Fixing her hair wasn't worth waiting in this line. She made her way upstairs to find one of the bathrooms or Buster, whichever came first.

There was a door at the end of the hall. She put her ear to it. She couldn't hear anything. She turned the knob and threw it open.

And at that moment, Jodi's heart fell in her chest like a keg of beer falling through the floor.

So. She'd found Buster and a bathroom, all at the same time. The problem was, he wasn't alone. There was a girl with him. She was topless. Buster's hands were on her big silicon boobs. He looked like he was checking two grapefruits for ripeness.

"Do you mind?" the girl yelled at Jodi. She clamped her hands over Buster's. She had buck teeth.

Buster turned to Jodi. His eyes widened.

"Buster," Jodi whispered.

"Oh, shit," Buster said.

"Who's that?" the girl asked.

"I'm Jodi."

"Uh—jeez, um, hey, Jodi," Buster stammered. His face turned pink. "This is Cindi."

"Mandi," the girl corrected him.

Jodi felt dizzy. She *knew* Mandi. Mandi had an IQ of four. She also had a boyfriend. Ken: the guy with the pool and the hot tub and the studio apartment. And where was he now? Jodi's eyes moved to Buster's cast and the new addition: Mandi's autograph, red heart dotting the *i* and all.

"Well, I think I'll be going now," Jodi said. Surprisingly, she wasn't even that angry. Maybe she was too shocked to be angry. Or maybe the overwhelming nausea she suddenly felt was preventing her from feeling anything other than a profound desire to either vomit or cry. And she didn't want Buster to witness either. That was for damn sure. So she turned and bolted back down the hall.

"Uh, wait," she heard Buster call after her. She hoped he would fall down and break his other leg. Or something else. The frat house spun around her. She felt like Alice in Wonderland—running as fast as she could, only to stay in the same place. It took her forever to get downstairs, with all the kids clustered on the stairs, drinking and making out. Even *Zack* was in her way—standing in front of a small crowd on the path in front of the house. Was he following her or something?

He was carrying an enormous plastic garbage bag full of something that smacked her on the shin.

"Sticky buns!" he shouted to the crowd. "Enough for all of us!"

Everybody cheered.

Jodi pushed past him. When she was a good hundred feet down the path, she looked behind her—but Buster was nowhere to be seen. He hadn't even followed her. She shivered. The night suddenly felt very cold, even though it was still the end of summer.

She ran another hundred feet and then sat down on a bench to catch her breath.

Was this really happening?

She took some big Lamaze-style breaths.

Wow. Buster had really moved on. The message was clear. It was as clear as if he had written it with the erasable Magic Marker attached by a string to the message board on her dorm door. So long, marriage. So long, house in East Quogue. So long, lobster boat.[21] So long to the perfect diamond engagement ring, which she had already picked out and which was on hold for her at Samuel's Jewelry Emporium in Great Neck. So long, going home together for Thanksgiving. So long, coffee milk shakes for breakfast and talking on the phone and going to the movies. And sex. *So long, sex—I'll miss you.* Jodi thought she would probably never have sex again.

□□□□□□□□□□□□□□□□□□□□□□□□□□□□□□□

21 Inside joke. Best thing about long-term relationships: inside jokes. So long, inside jokes.

It was at that moment, with Buster safely and snugly buried between Mandi's fake breasts in the disgusting Beta Phi Epsilon house, that Jodi finally began to cry. She wiped her eyes on Living La Vida Sofa.

So long, Buster.

Hello, triple. Hello, Celeste and Ali.

9

"Hey, you know what?" Jordan said. "I really don't feel like going to the Mint Julep Jamboree. Do you?"

Celeste could feel herself blushing for what must have been the millionth time tonight. She shook her head. She was having a great time—right here, right now, right in Jordan's room. She'd told him all about growing up in New York City, and he'd told her all about growing up in Iowa. He'd been to New York City only once. By coincidence, he had gone to Celeste's favorite place, too: the Cloisters. He'd picked a quince from a tree in the garden and had almost been arrested by a security guard. When Celeste had burst out laughing, he'd also mentioned that while most theologians asserted that Eve picked an apple in the Garden of Eden, it had really been a quince. Celeste had been speechless. Not only was Jordan handsome and brilliant and funny and endlessly fascinating, he also knew a lot about religion.

"I know of another cool party we can go to," Jordan said.

"Great," Celeste said.

A part of her couldn't help but feel a little disappointed, though. For one thing, she wasn't so great at parties. But more important, she'd been expecting him to suggest that they stay in his room. In all honesty, she'd been expecting him to make a move on her. Everything seemed to be leading up to it: the flirtatious talks about buying cookery for their dorms, the jokes about their favorite places to shop—and especially the game of pick-up sticks, which had ended with another outburst of delighted laughter.

"It's at the Brotherhood," Jordan said. He held the door open for her. He was so gentlemanly. Even his *room* was gentlemanly—with framed Matisse prints and pictures of his mom pinned to the corkboard above his desk. His roommate's side of the room was a mess, strewn with dirty laundry. The wall above his roommate's bed looked like a shrine to Britney Spears. This was probably exactly what that guy Buster's room looked like.

"What's the Brotherhood?" Celeste asked.

Jordan grinned. "It's an alternative frat," he said. "It's not in the Greek system."

"Oh," Celeste said.

They walked side by side in silence. Celeste kept waiting for him to take her hand. She left it dangling by her side, very deliberately. But he didn't notice.

The Brotherhood was pretty close to Jordan's dorm. It was an old renovated southern mansion—a lot nicer and better maintained than the frats she had seen so far. There was a banner above the door: We Do More Greek Than the Greeks.

Celeste didn't get it.

They walked into the house, and Jordan was immediately greeted by some of his friends. Celeste was shocked. How had he made friends so quickly? They even had some kind of secret handshake that happened so fast Celeste couldn't figure it out—except for a part in the middle where they turned around and bumped butts. It was so cute. They weren't kidding when they called themselves "the Brotherhood," either. Celeste was practically the only girl there. The place was filled with men—and actually, they were all really great looking.

Celeste sat down on a big overstuffed couch next to a potted ficus tree covered in sparkling white fairy lights. The couch was really comfortable and spotlessly white.

"Isn't that a great couch?" Jordan asked.

"Mm-hmm," Celeste said, looking deeply into his eyes.

"It's from Shabby Chic," he said.

Someone dressed as a butler was walking around with a tray of pink martinis, and Celeste took one. She took a sip. It was delicious.

"I like this martini," she said.

"That's because it's a cosmopolitan," Jordan said, smiling.

A cosmopolitan! Celeste thought dreamily. How very Dorothy-Parker-at-the-Algonquin. How very sophisticated-college-girl-out-with-her-boyfriend. She drank it down in about twenty seconds and then got another one. Her face grew flushed. A warm fuzziness spread in waves from her stomach. She was tipsy, and she liked it. This was practically the most she'd ever drunk.

Jordan leaned close to her. "You know, Celeste, you've got a killer style," he murmured. He smiled. "I *want* that shirt you're wearing."

"Uh . . . sure," she breathed.

Yes. As James Joyce would say: Yes, yes, yes, yes. This was it. The moment she'd been waiting for. *The move.* She knew it. She'd never had more fun with anybody. Maybe it was the cosmopolitans talking, but he might very well be the ONE. In which case, she had every intention of finally losing her virginity as soon as possible. Without thinking, or at least thinking less than usual, she leaned in and kissed Jordan. His lips were soft and warm, and he smelled delicious, like pink martinis and cologne. But he didn't seem particularly relaxed. She snuck a peek at him. His big blue eyes were open wide and staring right back at her.

Celeste pulled back. *Uh-oh.* Had she been too aggressive? How ironic! She'd never been aggressive in her life. About anything.

"Jordan? Is something wrong?"

"I like you, Celeste," he said. "The thing is . . ."

But before he could finish, one of the brothers yelled, "Bunny hop!" The next thing Celeste knew, Jordan was being whisked away, buried in a long line of men. Celeste tried to break into the line but couldn't. It was tighter than traffic on the West Side Highway. No one would let her in. *Oh, well.* She supposed she should let Jordan have his fun. He didn't seem like the frat type, but if he wanted to join a frat, this was as good a frat as any.

Celeste grabbed another cosmopolitan from the butler. She sank back into the couch. This one she sipped slowly and languorously, hoping to appear seductive, to lure Jordan back to her. But when she looked up again, Jordan had vanished.

All at once Celeste found herself drunkenly searching the house for him.

Where had he gone? What had happened to his gentlemanliness?

It was a good ten minutes before Celeste got her answer. Through a cracked doorway on the second floor, she saw him with one of his brothers in an oversized green velvet chair from Pottery Barn. But they weren't doing the secret handshake. Or even bumping butts. They were doing a hell of a lot more than that.

They were *kissing*.

No, they were passionately making out. Jordan was squeezing this guy as if he had just been handed the first quince in the Garden of Eden. And this time his eyes were closed. Tightly. His eyelids weren't even fluttering. *Oh my God!* How could she have been so stupid? When he'd told her that he wanted her shirt, she'd thought he'd wanted her to take it off. To be close to her. But that wasn't it at all.

Jordan was gay. He was as gay as they came.

It was so obvious now in retrospect. Jib and Carla had lots of gay friends, and *they* were all into Sartre and angel food cake and stylish clothes, too. But Celeste had been too caught up in his *kindness.* His *attentiveness.* She hadn't seen the forest for the trees. Ali and Jodi had hinted at this a couple of times, but Celeste had ignored them, thinking they were just jealous and therefore being rude. But they had just been trying to help. Of course they'd been trying to help! They'd been trying to prevent Celeste from completely humiliating herself and being branded a fool for the rest of her PU career. And clearly they'd failed. Correction: *she'd* failed.

Her throat tightened. Look at him! Jordan and his future husband hadn't even come up for air.

As Sartre would say: *Quelle disastre.*

When Celeste got back to the triple, Ali was deep in conversation on her cell phone with her DJ boyfriend, Sensei.

Ali was very upset. A half-eaten pizza from Little Italy Pizza and Subs lay in an open box on her bed. The Bible lay next to it, soaking wet and dyed orange. She had accidentally knocked a full can of orange Shasta on it. But that wasn't what was upsetting her. What was upsetting her was that Sensei was calling it quits.

"Wait, what?" Ali shouted into the phone. "We're breaking up."

"That's . . . I said . . . breaking up . . ."

"I *know* we're breaking up. I mean our *signal* is breaking up."

"Signal . . ." There was another burst of static.

Ali couldn't deal with this. Not now. She *needed* Sensei. Besides, he was the one who'd promised that the long-distance thing would work. He'd told her that they were destined to be reunited. True, he'd been burning a CD at the time and had been a little distracted, but . . .

She'd already had the worst night. For starters, she'd fallen asleep during her Bible study group and had been asked to leave. It wasn't her fault she had fallen asleep. Someone had made pitchers of Bloody Marys to enjoy during the Bible discussion, and Bloody Marys made her sleepy. Probably all the sodium. She must have been the first person in the history of the Christian rave scene to be asked to leave. Jesus Christ! The whole *point* of the Christian rave scene was that no one was ever asked to leave.

So then she had wandered, dejected, around campus for two hours. She'd ended up at the ComServ Rally 'Round the Lake, where she had signed up to work at the animal shelter a few times a week. She figured, why not do community service? Animals were the only ones who understood her, anyway. Animals and Sensei. At least, that was what she'd always assumed.

"I don't understand why this is happening, Sensei," Ali pleaded into her cell phone. "Just tell me what's going on. I need an answer."

Just then Jodi walked into the room. She glanced at Celeste. Celeste shrugged.

Ali frowned. The two of them were just standing there. Couldn't they tell that this was a private, personal conversation? She turned away from them and tried to concentrate on what Sensei was saying. Once again she could only make out every other word or so. It was like talking in Morse code.

"The. Have. Aligned. Led. To. Soul. A. Woman. Blossom. DJs. This. Called. And . . ."

"Wait," Ali said, so frustrated and upset she was practically in tears. "I can't understand you. Say that again."

"Stars. All. And. Me. My. Mate. Beautiful. Named. Who. At. Club. Sapphire . . ."

Suddenly Ali figured it out. "The stars have aligned and led you to your soul mate? A beautiful woman named Blossom who DJs at a club called Sapphire?"

"Yes. *Bzzzt . . . bzzzt.* She . . . "

"She *what?*" Ali shrieked. "What does she do?"

Bzzzt . . . click.

"Hello? Sensei? Hello?"

The line was dead.

Ali paused for a moment in sad shock. She couldn't believe this. How could you have closure on a relationship when your last word to the guy was "hello"? She looked at her two roommates. "I've just been dumped," she announced. "For a woman. Yes, *woman.*" Her voice took on an edge. "Named Blossom. Yes, *Blossom.*"

Jodi sniffed.

"What's the matter with *you?*" Ali demanded.

"I was dumped for a girl named Mandi," Jodi said. "With an *i.*" She was almost tempted to change her name to Irma or Mildred or Barb. Even Josie would be better.

Celeste laughed miserably.

"What's so funny?" Jodi and Ali asked at the exact same time, so that Celeste heard their voices in stereo.

"At least you weren't dumped for a man," Celeste said.

Ali and Jodi looked at each other. Then they looked back at Celeste.

And then they all did what they simultaneously realized roommates are supposed to do. They laughed hysterically for about ten minutes, until they ended up crying.

10

Jodi was the first to get a grip on herself.

"What's wrong with me?" she asked, sniffling. "How could I be so stupid? I really thought I was going to be with Buster forever."

The reality of what had just happened hit her all over again and she got very quiet.

"So here we are, all three of us, dumped," Ali said.

"Unbelievable," Celeste murmured. "It's so Edith Wharton."

For some reason, the comments annoyed Jodi. "I don't think you guys can compare what happened to you to what happened to me," she said. "I've been in love with Buster since middle school. For *six* years. One third of my entire life. We were going to get *married.* I don't think you can compare that to a date with a fag or a long-distance relationship breaking up. Everyone knows that all long-distance relationships break up." Jodi's voice caught in her throat. Her eyes watered. "And I don't have any clothes, or money, or hair products. And I have to *work.*

And I was the one who loved college more than anybody. . . ."

"You're right, Jodi, I'm sorry," Celeste said. She sat beside Jodi on Jodi's bed and gave her an awkward hug. "I just meant, you know, we're all really bummed out."

"I know. I'm sorry, too," Jodi said, sort of clinging to Celeste's arm.

Ali arched an eyebrow. "You two aren't going to push your beds together again, are you?" she asked sarcastically.

Jodi laughed through her tears.

"Jodi, we'll give you clothes," Celeste offered. "We can all share stuff."

"But dude, you have to promise to burn that Living La Vida Sofa T-shirt," Ali said.

"Done." Jodi blew her nose into one of the Little Italy napkins. "You guys want to know something pathetic? I've never even been with anyone other than Buster. He's the only guy I've ever had sex with."

"You're kidding," Ali said. She decided not to add "eeew."

"Well, I've never even had sex with anyone," Celeste admitted. She grabbed a slice of pizza from Ali's box and ate a big piece of sausage.

Ali's eyes widened. "Whoa, dude," she said.

"We need to drink more," Jodi said.

"Let's make cosmopolitans," Celeste suggested.

Jodi took a look around their pitiful little room. "We don't have anything to make them with," she said, on the verge of crying again. "We don't even have beer."

Ali grinned. "We have Jib's pot."

"Be my guests," Celeste said.

In less than a minute, Ali had rolled a joint, lit it, and passed it to Jodi. Celeste declined.

"Well, at least we're not the only losers," Jodi said, holding a big puff of pot smoke in her lungs. "There's lazy-eyed, narcoleptic K. J. Martin next door and her roommate, Hallie."

"Hallie Tosis,[22]" Ali added.

The two of them giggled.

There was a knock on their door.

"Who is it?" Celeste called nervously. She might be miserable, but she didn't exactly relish the thought of getting kicked out of college for drugs before classes had even started.

"Your neighbors," a high-pitched voice with an English accent answered.

Jodi and Ali giggled again. *Right on cue,* they both thought.

Lazy-eyed, narcoleptic K. J. Martin and Hallie Tosis burst into the room. They were staggering a little. Jodi, Ali, and Celeste let out a collective gasp. The girls weren't alone. These two losers were actually with two *guys.*

"Oh my God," Jodi said. All at once she felt like crying again. Maybe it was the pot, but the guys seemed cute in a Busterish kind of way: frat-boy hotties in baggy khaki pants and PU T-shirts. They looked like twins.

"Do you people have any more of that great-smelling

22 Real name: Hallie Thompson.

weed?" lazy-eyed, narcoleptic K. J. Martin asked. "We'll trade you this for it." She held up a nearly full bottle of tequila.

Jodi and Ali looked to Celeste. Technically it was her pot, after all.

Celeste shrugged.

Jodi stubbed out the joint and handed it to Hallie Tosis. "Here," she said. "It's barely been touched. And it's good. Very good."

"Thanks, Jodi, you're a *superstah,*" Hallie Tosis said. Hallie was always calling everyone a *superstah* in her English accent and breathing on everyone when she got to the *stah* part. She had terrible breath. Hence her name.

The little foursome scurried next door to their room.

"Do you think all four of them are actually going to do it in there?" Celeste asked.

"It's too disgusting to think about," Ali mumbled. She cracked open the bottle and took a big slug. "Ugh. Straight tequila is hard to swallow."

Jodi wiped her eyes. The urge to cry had passed. If her neighbors were getting some nookie, fine. She shouldn't feel sorry for herself because of it. She should take action. Yes, it was time to do something to forget all about the heinous bullshit that had happened in the last week. The problem was, aside from the booze, they had absolutely nothing to occupy themselves with except each other. Jodi scanned the room. Her eyes came to rest on her closet. Actually, that wasn't quite true.

"Well, girls, at least we have Scrabble," she said dryly. She stood and grabbed her grandmother's present, then sat with it on the floor. "If we're going to be the biggest losers on campus, we might as well go for it all the way."

Ali and Celeste both smiled, then joined her. They ripped open the shrink-wrapped box, laid the board on the linoleum, and turned over all the pieces. They selected their letters and put them in their letter racks. Then they each took a sip of tequila. Ali was right. It *was* hard to swallow.

"Who's first, y'all?" Ali asked.

"I'll go," Celeste said. She carefully spelled out the word *cat*. "Four points."

"Okay, okay, wait a minute." Jodi shook her head. "We have to at least try to make this a little more interesting. I say—"

A loud, muffled moan cut her off. It came from the other side of the wall.

The three girls froze.

"That's so good, baby." It was lazy-eyed, narcoleptic K. J. Martin. Her voice rang out as if she were in the room with them—only muted, as if she were wearing a gas mask.

"Yes, Nigel. Yes, yes! You're a super*stah!*" followed.

"My name is not Nigel," they heard through the wall. "It's Hank."

"I don't care what your bloody name is! You're a super*stah!*"

Jodi, Ali, and Celeste each took a big swig of booze. Then Ali jumped up and ran over to the clock radio by her bedside table. She turned it on and cranked up the volume. The song was "Give It Away Now," by the Red Hot Chili Peppers. It sounded very tinny and distorted. But it was a hell of a lot better than listening to what was going on next door.

"Nigel?" Jodi muttered.

"I've never done it with a Nigel," Ali said, sitting back down. "I've done it with a Quentin, but never a Nigel."

"Hey, that gives me an idea!" Jodi exclaimed. "How about we only use boys' names and swearwords from now on?"

Ali clapped. "Right on, y'all!" she exclaimed.

"Does my *cat* still count?" Celeste asked.

"Only if you change it to *pussy*," Jodi said.

Celeste pursed her lips. "Eeew. I hate that word."

Ali used the *t* in *cat* and put down an *o* and an *m*. "*Tom*," she said. "Three points."

Jodi used the *m* in *Tom* to make *mother*.

"*Mother?*" Ali asked. "That's not a boy's name *or* a swear-word."

"It's short for *motherfucker*," Jodi said.

The three of them laughed and drank more tequila. Amazingly, they were actually starting to feel better. "Give It Away Now" ended. "You Shook Me All Night Long," by AC/DC, was next.

"Do you think those girls next door are requesting these songs?" Ali mumbled.

"*Hank, you shook me a-a-a-l-l n-i-i-ight l-o-o-ong!*" Jodi sang in a very out-of-key voice.

Celeste giggled. She put down an *o*, a *c*, and a *k*—building on her own *c* in *cat* to form *cock*. "Great. I've been dying to make *cock*."

"Kinky," Jodi said. She turned to Ali. "Hey, did you really do it with a Quentin? I'm not sure I believe you."

"It's all true, dude. Actually, I've done it with a Quentin and I've also done it with a Quinn." She winked. "The Mighty Quinn."

"*Two* guys with names starting with *Q?*" Celeste asked. She was stunned. Ali was unbelievable. What had Celeste been doing with herself her entire life? Actually, she knew the answer. She'd been hiding in her apartment on the Upper West Side, reading about people who led fabulous lives and went on fabulous adventures and slept with fabulous people. But Ali was out there actually *doing* it. In more ways than one.

"You know, y'all, there's a lot of guys out there in the world," Ali said. "With a lot of names. There's millions of guys all over the world for all twenty-six letters of the alphabet. In fact, I bet there's at least a dozen guys for each letter of the alphabet right here at Pollard."

All three girls pondered this profound thought for a moment.

"Hey, I got an idea," Ali said. She stood up again and stepped to her desk to get three pieces of paper. "Make a list of all the guys you've done it with—" She stopped in midsentence, remembering that Celeste had never done it, period, and Jodi had only done it with Buster. ". . . I mean kissed. Make a list of all the guys you've kissed."

Neither Celeste nor Jodi knew where Ali was going with this, but they got to work anyway with their little Scrabble pencils.

When they were all finished, they compared lists. Between them they'd racked up, among others, five Mikes, three Johns, and, of course, one Quentin. The tally was truly woeful for Celeste: seven, which included five from a sixth-grade spin-the-bottle party. Josh, Steven, Evan, Peter, William, Edward, and Jordan . . . if Jordan even counted. Two *E's,* two *J's,* a *P,* an *S,* and a *W.* Jodi had fourteen, if she counted her second cousin, "All Hands" Teddy. Ali had a mind-boggling thirty-four. She had written them down in order from *A* to *Z,* and only two letters were left without boys' names next to them. Ali had never been with a *B* or an *X.*

"I should do something about that," Ali said. "*B* should be easy, but the *X*-man will probably be a little harder."

"Unless you meet Zorro," Celeste said.

Ali grinned. "You're drunk. Zorro starts with a *Z,* not an *X.* And you're the one who will probably meet Zorro—the *Gay* Blade."

Celeste frowned, but she ended up laughing. Ali was right. She *was* drunk. "I want to catch up with you guys," she said, comparing her sad little list to theirs.

"Well, why don't we all start from the top?" Jodi suggested. "We'll prove to ourselves that we don't need just one guy to make us happy. Especially if that guy is (*a*) gay, (*b*) dating some loser named Blossom, or (*c*) the biggest asshole on the planet. There are plenty of *T's, D's,* and *H's* out there. Toms, Dicks, and

Harrys. We should each kiss one guy for every letter of the alphabet. That'll show Buster and Jordan and Samsung."

"Sensei," Ali corrected. As if it even mattered. The idea sounded intriguing. In fact, it sounded like the best idea Ali had heard in a long time. Way better than Christian raving. "I think we should have to have sex with them."

Celeste looked mortified.

Jodi shook her head. "We're not skanks," she said. "A kiss—a real French kiss—is enough. And they have to kiss you back. With feeling."

"So it's like a contest?" Celeste asked. She was suddenly happy. The horrible events of the recent past had melted into this happy, tequila-soaked, hazy night with the girls.

Ali sat up straight, sharing Celeste's excitement. "Whoever kisses all the letters in the alphabet first wins a prize," she said.

"In order!" Jodi exclaimed, catching the thrill of it.

"Okay, in order. From *A* to *Z*," Ali agreed. "From Adam to Zane. From Alex to Zack."

Jodi thought of crazy kitchen-man, wild-haired Zack. She'd have to find another *Z*. Or maybe she could use him in a worst-case scenario. It wouldn't be *so* bad. . . . "I'm in," Celeste said.

"Me too," said Jodi.

"Me three," said Ali.

They all put their hands together over the Scrabble board and laughed. Celeste caught a glimpse of her watch. It was nearly three A.M.

"Oh, man," she moaned. "I should go to sleep. I have a nine A.M. class."

She couldn't believe that it was already the first day of classes. Orientation week had gone by so fast. In just a few hours, college was going to really begin.

"Hey, what are we going to call the competition?" Jodi asked.

"How about Dudes from *A* to *Z?*" Ali offered.

"How about Adam to Zechariah?" Celeste wondered out loud. She was trying to keep it biblical. It made her feel less dirty somehow.

Jodi thought for a minute. "How about the Alphabetical Hookup List?" she suggested.

Ali and Celeste looked at each other. Their faces lit up. They each took one last sip and toasted the name. It was settled.

"So tomorrow let's all go out there, work hard, and earn those *A*'s," Jodi said, winking.

Ali and Celeste laughed.

"Let's all get *A*'s," Ali said.

"Get those *A*'s!" Celeste joined in.

But none of them were talking about good grades.

11

The next morning Jodi called the mail room about her belongings. Still no word, of course. It had become part of the routine of college life: *Where the hell is my shit? We have no idea, ma'am. Click.* Luckily her roommates came through for her—Celeste with a plain blue skirt and Ali with a long-sleeved black-and-white-striped T-shirt. It felt great to be wearing normal clothes again. She'd been way too harsh in judging her roommates' respective wardrobes. It really wasn't a bad little outfit.

After thanking them profusely, Jodi ran to Blue Sky Coffee on Broad Street to grab a quick frozen mochaccino[23] before class. Unfortunately, she forgot that she didn't have any money.

Kitchen-duty payday was Friday. She was trying to convince the townie behind the counter to run a tab for her when someone tapped her on the shoulder. It was a guy with zits

---

23 Second-best cure for a hangover.

all over his face. Jodi almost retched. It was way too early in the morning to be reminded of Ali's cold leftover pizza.

"I'm Alex Cronin," the guy said. "We're in Contemporary Civilization together. We met on line at registration."

Jodi had no memory of the incident at all. But she really didn't care. Zit-faced Alex started with *A*. Or did it start with *Z?*

"Look, if you're having trouble paying for that, I'd be happy to pick up the bill," zit-faced Alex said. His voice was filled with pride, as if he had just offered to pay her entire tuition.

"Oh, thank you. I'll pay you back," Jodi said. *With a big French kiss right here,* she thought.

"That won't be necessary. How much is it?" zit-faced Alex asked the counter boy. "Four ninety-five? Whew. That's some pricey drink you ordered . . ." He looked at her.

"Jodi," she said.

"Well, no problem, Jodi. It's my pleasure." Zit-faced A-man handed over a five-dollar bill. He didn't look too happy about it.

"Thank you so much, Alex," Jodi said, shoving a straw in the slit of the plastic lid and taking a frosty sip. She felt better already.

"Oh, please don't mention it."

"Let the games begin," Jodi murmured to herself.

Zit-faced Alex smiled at her. "What? Oh, you mean classes. First day of school and all that. Right. Let the games begin! Rah rah rah, sis boom bah!"

Jodi laughed. She didn't think she'd ever met a bigger

loser in her life. Best just to get this over with. "So anyway, thanks again," she said. She put her iced mochaccino down on a table, grabbed zit-faced Alex with both of her hands on his shoulders, and kissed him square on the mouth.

He kissed her right back.

Score one for Jodi!

So what if her first kiss since Buster was with this zit-faced guy? It was good that he was ugly. That was the whole point. He was her *A,* and that was all that mattered.

Jodi made a mental note to discuss exactly how long the kiss had to be with Ali and Celeste. She had learned on *Oprah* that you should sing the entire song "Happy Birthday to You" slowly while washing your hands after using a public rest room, to make sure you had killed all the germs. She tried it now, but "Happy Birthday to You" was pretty long. She counted to three instead and then cut the kiss off.

"Wow," zit-faced Alex breathed. His jaw was slack. His eyes were wide.

It was strangely liberating. There really were millions of men out there, and Jodi could kiss any one of them if she wanted to. Without so much as a good-bye, she took another sip of mochaccino to wash away the taste of zit-faced Alex and left for class.

She froze right outside the door.

There was Buster, standing right across the street with some of his new best Beta Phi Whiffle Ball friends. He was wearing his What Part of www.youareafuckingasshole.com Don't You Understand? T-shirt. Yesterday she would have thought it was cute. Now she just wanted to throw the rest of the mochaccino onto it.

But wait.

Buster began with *B.* Jodi smiled. Of course. As Celeste's dad might say, this wasn't coincidence; it was karma. Buster pretended not to see her—the fucking coward—but she marched straight over to him, grabbed him, and kissed him for a complete (albeit fast) silent version of "Happy Birthday to You"—inserting the line "dear Shitbag" in place of "dear Buster." Then she pulled away and slapped him as hard as she could across his smug, square-jawed face. It nearly knocked him off his crutches.

His friends burst out laughing.

"Dude!" one of them yelled. It was the smartest comment any of them could muster.

"Hey, wha-wha-what was that all about?" Buster stammered.

"What part of it don't you understand?" she snapped. She took a deep breath and strolled down the sidewalk toward campus. For some reason, she began thinking about the time she and Buster had gone on a field trip to the Metropolitan Museum of Art in New York City with Señora Hernandez's tenth-grade Spanish class. They had been on their way to the Basque art exhibit, walking through this huge hall of gigantic paintings of Jesus on the cross, when all of a sudden Buster ripped an incredibly loud fart. It had echoed like rolling thunder down the stone walls and marble floor. Everyone had turned and stared at him. And he'd laughed.

"Hey, what do you want? I just ate ham. I think I have ham poisoning."

"Jamón!" Señora Hernandez had instructed.

Jodi shuddered, remembering the scene. *Jamón* was pretty much the only Spanish word she remembered now. How could she ever forget it? And this was the guy she was pining for? A museum farter? As Señora Hernandez always used to say, "No way, José."

It was definitely time to move on, and that was exactly what she was doing. And as far as the Alphabetical Hookup List was concerned, she was off to a great start. *A* and *B* were already *finito,* and it wasn't even nine A.M.

Celeste was having a little more trouble getting started.

It wasn't until her second class, Intro to Psych—the infamous Psych 101, to be exact—that she finally got down to business. Her first class, French, had just whizzed by. She had to admit she'd been in sort of a daze the whole time. The teacher . . . at this moment Celeste couldn't even remember his name, Monsieur something or other . . . had held the class outside in the field. They'd sat in a circle in the grass, and Celeste had been so nervous and so happy (this was exactly how she had pictured it would be in college, sitting in a circle outside—more of a *workshop* than a class) that she hadn't been able to concentrate. Especially since she was wearing a short skirt and she'd been trying to make sure her underwear didn't show. Sitting Indian-style had been out of the question. So had listening for the names of any boys that started with *A*.

The only thing she really remembered was the teacher—no, *professor*—saying, *"Au revoir."*

But now she was ready for action.

The psych professor wrote his name in big letters on the blackboard: *Prof. A. Simon.*

Celeste grinned. *A?* Ha! She could just picture *that* scenario. She, willing to do anything to earn her *A,* would approach the teacher, Prof. A. Simon, after class, and say, "Oh, Professor Simon, I would do anything to get an *A* in this class. Anything. What can I do for extra credit?"

"You can make love to me right here and now," Professor A. Simon would say.

Then she would bounce up on his big desk and they'd kiss passionately. "Oh, Professor," she'd murmur. She could do it. She had read *Lolita.* The professor would ravish her on the desk—

"Celeste Alexander," Professor Simon shouted for the third time, finally snapping Celeste out of her fantasy. "Are you here or aren't you?"

"Present!" Celeste called without thinking. She felt herself blush.

Everybody stared at her.

"Are you feeling okay?" Professor Simon asked, peering over his little round glasses.

"Yes, fine, thank you," Celeste mumbled. How could she have even thought of kissing him, with his shiny bald head and his three little sprouts of hair? She felt like crawling under her chair and hiding. Maybe she should have deferred. Just taken a year off to travel around Europe first. How embarrassing to be asked if you're okay, especially in a *psych* class. She slumped down in her chair and listened to the rest of attendance, her pen carefully poised to write down the names of any boys beginning with *A*.

"Jordan Cole," Professor Simon called next.

Celeste stiffened. She cast a surreptitious glance around the classroom, but he wasn't there. *Thank God.* Maybe he had dropped the class. She couldn't bear the thought of see-ing Jordan day in and day out as Professor Simon lectured the class about repression and sexuality and transference and all sorts of other painfully relevant issues. Besides, at this moment she wasn't even here to learn. Well, she *was,* of course—but she was also here to get started on her list. She was going to show her roommates that she wasn't the shel-tered little girl they imagined her to be. No sirree.

In a class of about forty kids, there were lots of choices for the letter *A:* Andrew Eagan, Alerick Kane, Arden Smith, and Arthur Stewart.

Arthur Stewart looked familiar. How did she know him? He was tall and cute. She decided she would try to talk to him after class. Another of the *A*'s, Andrew, was sitting right in front of her. She hadn't seen his face, but he looked a little chunky. He seemed like one of those sweater boys who always wore a turtleneck sweater. He wasn't wearing one now because it was way too hot, but she knew that he would as soon as it was cool enough. He also seemed sort of, well, uncomfortable. He kept shifting around and sneezing, then wiping his nose on a wadded-up paper towel he had in his shorts pocket. Celeste tried to ignore it, but it was kind of grossing her out. She would definitely stick with Arthur Stewart.

She spent the rest of the class figuring out how best to approach him.[24] In the end, she decided on a simple, non-committal, nonthreatening "Hi, mind if I talk to you for a second?"

As soon as class was dismissed, Celeste summoned her courage and followed Arthur out the door and into the hall. She tapped him on the shoulder. He turned around and smiled, looking more familiar than ever. How did she know him? From back home, maybe? She stared at his face, but she just couldn't remember.

"Yes?" he asked.

"Uh . . . hi—oh, hi," Celeste stuttered. She swallowed. "Mind if I . . . well, I wanted to talk to you about something for a second." Her face felt hot.

Arthur laughed. "Why? Is there food caught in my teeth or something?"

Celeste was mortified. "No!"

"Good. You had me worried there for a second."

Celeste shook her head. This wasn't going according to plan. Not at all. "I'm sorry, you look familiar, that's all. I'm Celeste Alexander. Your name is Arthur, isn't it?"

He nodded. "But I like to be called Artha," he said. "Ar-tha."

□□□□□□□□□□□□□□□□□□□□□□□□□□□□□□□

24 Professor Simon discussed, among other things, the basic definitions of narcissism and solipsism—but Celeste was much too involved with her own problems to pay any attention.

"You do? Why?" Celeste's eyes narrowed. She wondered if he was playing a joke on her.

"Because it rhymes with Martha. Get it? Ar-tha Stewart." He laughed again.

Suddenly Celeste remembered where she'd seen him. An image of him surrounded by pea green velvet flashed through her mind. *Oh my God.* He was the guy kissing Jordan in the Pottery Barn chair. *Him.* Of course. Artha Stewart? How much more gay could you get? She started backing away from him and ended up slamming into somebody. She whirled around.

"Excuse me, I'm sor—" She broke off.

It was Jordan.

"I can't believe I missed the class," Jordan said breezily. "I'm in financial aid hell. I was in that office for over an hour."

Celeste cringed. As Hallie Tosis would say, "Shite." She would have to make a trip to the Drop/Add office as soon as possible.

Jordan smiled at Artha, then back at Celeste. "Oh, good!" he exclaimed. "Have you two met?"

Artha nodded. "I was admiring her skirt. I have trousers in a pattern just like it."

Celeste shuddered. *Trousers.* Who said "trousers"? She felt as though she had accidentally wandered into a bad episode of *Will & Grace.*

"We have to make a time to get together," Jordan said to her.

"Okay," Celeste said miserably.

Jordan kissed Artha on the cheek, then the two of them walked off, holding hands. Celeste stared at their butts as they disappeared down the hall. *Quelle embarrassment.*

Somebody cleared his throat beside her.

Celeste turned and saw Andrew, the chunky guy who kept sneezing.

"Uh, hi," he said. "I couldn't help notice that you were looking at me in class." He smiled the same way Artha had smiled. "I was just worried that I had something on the back of my shirt."

Celeste gave him a quick once-over. Face-to-face, he wasn't that bad looking, just kind of bloated—with puffy eyelids and puffy cheeks and puffy knuckles.

"Your name is Celeste, right?" Andrew the Bloated asked.

She nodded. *Seize the* A, she thought. "Yeah," she said. "And you're Andrew, right?"

"Andy," Andy the Bloated said. All at once his face scrunched up, and he sneezed again, almost in Celeste's face. "Sorry," he said. He blew his nose in the wadded-up paper towel. "Allergies. These old classrooms are so dusty."

"Hey . . . I was wondering," Celeste began. "You know, I wasn't really paying attention in there. And I was just thinking, maybe I could borrow your notes. You know, we could get together *today* for lunch or something." She really emphasized the word *today*.

"Uh, uh . . ." His face turned red. He stared down at his bloated sneakers. "Well, I'd really like to, Celeste, but here's the problem. . . ."

Oh my God. He was saying no. Something about a girl-friend back home. A promise they had made to each other one day in an apple orchard. As if she cared. This was a new low point. It was one thing being rejected by a guy who was gay. That was understandable. But to have a big bloated boy with allergies tell her about a girlfriend, that was something else entirely. *That* was pathetic.

Oh, well. There were other *A*'s in the sea. Supposedly, anyway.

The last thing on Ali's mind was the hookup game, or what-ever they were calling it. She'd have plenty of time to worry about that later. The way she figured it, winning would be easy. She simply needed two things: the student directory and one full day. Maybe two. At most. But right now—as she sat alone in the quad and stuffed her face with a sausage pizza[25]—all she could think about was the bad time she was having. Her classes weren't really what she'd expected. They were no different from her high school classes. She had thought that the setting would involve more of an "equal exchange of ideas"—which was how classes were advertised in the catalog.

As she was quickly discovering, the catalog was full of shit.

Take her first class of the day. She had signed up for a writing course with the playwright David Mamet. That's what it said in the catalog: David Mamet. But when she'd gotten

---

25 She would also have plenty of time later to worry about the Freshman Fifteen.

to the classroom, David Mamet was nowhere to be seen. The real instructor—a gangly, long-haired guy named Shapiro—had just laughed at her and said, "Sorry to disappoint you, but did you really think that David Mamet would actually be here? Why the hell would David Mamet be *here?* He's in Hollywood, baby. Or in New York. But he sure ain't here."

"But it said in the catalog—"

"I don't care what it said in the catalog. If it said the queen of England was teaching Home Ec, would you believe that, too? First rule of writing: Try having some common sense. Maybe if you're lucky, David Mamet will show up and read something for about fifteen minutes. But I wouldn't hold my breath if I were you."

Ali had spent the rest of the class fighting back tears.

She took another bite of pizza. All around her kids were laughing happily and talking and rushing off to places together. It was so big and confusing and scary here. She'd only had one nice moment all day—when she'd run into Celeste and Jodi on the long line at the Drop/Add office. It had been great to see a couple of friendly faces and make little *"A"* hand signals at each other. If it weren't for her roomies, she'd have been completely alone. . . .

A sign taped to the fountain caught her eye.

FIRST MEETING OF THE LESBIAN ALLIANCE
TOMORROW NIGHT

Now *that* was something you didn't see in high school. At least where *she* had gone to high school. Ali didn't really even know that many lesbians. She'd never had a girl-girl experience, but she had sort of always wondered about switch-hitting. There wasn't any harm in checking it out. Hey, after all, that's what college was all about—experimenting, broadening your horizons, learning what it was like on the other side of the fence.

Ali grinned. She stood up and approached the sign, glancing at her watch. The meeting was taking place in the Jefferson Davis wing of the Allween Library.

A girl walked up beside her.

"Are you going to that meeting?" the girl asked.

"I was thinking about it," Ali said.

"Great!" She stuck out her hand. (At least, Ali was pretty sure she was a "she." She was very big and muscular, with a platinum blond crew cut, and she was wearing what looked like a maintenance man's uniform—complete with a belt that had dozens of keys.) "My name is Barbara. I'm a senior, and I'm president of the Lesbian Alliance. And this is the year we're going to finally found our own house—the Sisterhood of the Brotherhood."

Ali smiled and shook her hand. "Cool. My name's Ali."

Barbara bent forward and kissed her on the cheek.

Wow. Barbara continued talking, but Ali couldn't listen. All she could think about was how cool Barbara seemed to be. Hanging out with her would be a hell of a lot better than the Christian raves, and it would certainly be more interesting than sitting in Dimers and drinking backwash. Definitely. If anything was going to suit Ali, it was being a lesbian. She could tell already.

12

Jodi went to work that night feeling a little more upbeat and confident. Not that she wanted to be there, especially on BBQ night. *Au contraire.* Just the smell alone . . . but she was sure she had figured out the trick to winning this whole alphabetical hookup thing. She was calling her method "the Surprise Attack." It was self-explanatory. Grab a guy, start making out with him, then run away. Raging testosterone in males aged eighteen to twenty-two ensured that they'd kiss back, unless they happened to be in the Brotherhood.

So as soon as she burst through the big double doors to the kitchen, she marched right up to Charlie,[26] who worked the deep-fat fryer, and kissed him long and hard.

"Thank you," Charlie whimpered.

"No, thank *you*," Jodi said.

Suddenly Lips, an old guy with the big rubbery lips and

---

26 Served three years for credit card fraud; currently out on parole.

deranged eyes who ran the kitchen, stomped in and started yelling at everyone.

"Someone is stealing food! Do you hear me? And when you steal food from my kitchen, you rip the heart right out of my chest and eat it."

"Eeew," Jodi whispered.

"I demand to know who stole my sticky buns!" Lips barked. "I came in for the breakfast shift and what did I see?"

"No sticky buns?" Zack asked, winking at Jodi.

Lips spun around and pointed a long-handled ladle at him. "Was it you, Mr. Hippie?"

Zack rolled his eyes. He reached into the pocket of his barbecue-sauce-stained apron and dug out a pack of cigaril-los. "First of all, my name is not Mr. Hippie. I'm an *intellectual,* not a hippie. Second, we are *allowed* to take dessert home with us." He lit up and blew out a big cloud of smoke. "It's in the manual. And last night I had a sweet tooth."

"Don't smoke in here!" Lips shouted, his scrawny face red with rage.

Jodi laughed. It was kind of sweet, the way Zack owned up to stealing the sticky buns. He might be a criminal, but at least he was an honest one—unlike the rest of the felons she worked with. And he was sort of funny . . . in a very, very off-kilter kind of way.

"Hey, Lips, what's your real name?" Jodi asked.

"That's none of your business," Lips snapped, turning the ladle on her.

"Sorry," Jodi mumbled. She was really itching for a *D,* but she supposed she'd have to wait. There was Gross Fredo, who chopped and diced things, but she needed *D* and *E* first. Hey, maybe she could call him Dicing and Chopping Gross Fredo and that would be her *D*. But no, that wasn't really his name. That would be cheating. And in the wake of Zack's confession, she felt a strange but powerful need to win this game honestly.

"Things are going to be different around here from now on," Lips said. "For one thing, starting tomorrow, you have to wear a hair net at all times when you're in the kitchen. I'm getting a shipment of hair nets." He was waving the ladle at Zack again. "And thanks to *you,* we're going to have much stricter rules about taking dessert home. From now on, you are only allowed to take one piece of fruit at the end of the shift. No baked goods, no boxes of cereal, no hamburgers— just one piece of fruit."

"Fine, Lips," Zack said. "What you don't understand is that nobody cares."

They got to work, spooning up ribs and black-eyed peas and collard greens. Zack amused everyone by talking in a southern accent, even though he was from New Jersey. About fifteen minutes into the shift Jodi realized a couple of things. One: She was having a pretty good time. Two: She hadn't thought about Buster once.

"I think I'm gonna split early tonight," Zack suddenly announced. "It's been nice slaving with you." He headed for the door, then paused. "Whoops, I almost forgot my *one* piece of fruit." He grabbed an entire watermelon off the shelf and hobbled out the kitchen, grunting under the weight.

Jodi giggled as she watched him go. Come to think of it, she was pretty hungry herself. And she didn't feel much like hanging around here anymore, either. If Zack could leave early, so could she.

She took a quick look around. Lips was nowhere to be seen. Then she spotted an industrial-size can of Campbell's alphabet soup high up on a shelf. Campbell's alphabet soup was tomato based wasn't it? Yes. Of course it was. And she'd learned long ago that, contrary to popular belief, the tomato was a fruit, not a vegetable. (Something to do with the seeds.) So grabbing that can of tomato soup would sort of be like taking one piece of fruit.

Good. It was settled.

She grabbed the can and headed home to her room.

The soup was a big hit back at the triple. All three of them had a bowl. Jodi fished an *A* out of her soup with the tip of her spoon and let it slide down her throat. She tried eating the soup the way she had when she was a little girl, alphabetically. Celeste tried to spell words until she ran out of vowels. Ali was a little hesitant at first. She frowned at the little saucepan as it bubbled on the hot plate.

"What's wrong?" Jodi asked.

"I can't fully enjoy alphabet soup without crumbling Ritz crackers into it," Ali said. But she poured herself a steaming bowl, anyway.

Celeste laughed nervously. "You know, you guys, it's illegal to have a hot plate in the dorm," she said.

Jodi rolled her eyes. "It's also illegal to stash pot in your dorm, but we're not gonna turn you in," she said.

Celeste blushed.

"So how's everyone doing with the AHUL?" Jodi asked.

"The what?" Ali asked.

"The Alphabetical Hookup List," Jodi said.

"Oh, great," Ali said.

"Me too," Jodi said.

"Me too," Celeste lied.

Jodi absently fiddled with her letters, stirring them in her bowl. "I have a question about the rules," she said. "How long do we have to actually kiss the guy for?"

"I don't think we can put a time minimum on it exactly," Ali said. "It just has to be a real kiss. Mutual. And with tongue."

Jodi nodded. "So we're leaving the length of the kiss up to the kisser's discretion. You just have to be honest about it."

"I think a lot of this has to be on the honor system," Celeste agreed.

"I think we better put a ten-second minimum on the kiss," Ali said. She kissed the back of her own hand passionately, counting to ten in her mind. "On second thought, that's long. Let's make it seven seconds."

"How old are we, ten?" Jodi asked, giggling. "We're sitting around eating ABC soup and kissing the backs of our hands. Why don't we practice making out with our pillows next?"

"I was timing myself," Ali said.

"How about we say you have to sing the entire alphabet song in your head during the kiss?" Jodi said.

"Including *now I know my ABCs, next time won't you sing with me?*" Celeste asked. She wondered how in the hell she was going to kiss a guy and sing the alphabet at the same time. Wouldn't she have other things on her mind, like if she was kissing correctly? There were a lot of things to worry about when you kissed a guy, like relaxing your jaw but not relaxing it *too* much. Celeste was always worried that a guy would be able to hear her jaw click.

"Has anyone here ever BEEN with a girl?" Ali asked.

Jodi scowled. "Eeew. Are you kidding? Never. Although I did make out at a party once with Buster and another girl, sort of a truth-or-dare thing. It was a ménage à make out. But I only did that because I was totally hammered."

Celeste shook her head, mildly horrified. She'd never even held another girl's hand.

"I've never been with a girl, either," Ali said. "But I think it might be interesting. They say only a woman knows what another woman wants."

"Are we going to push the beds together again?" Celeste joked.

The other two laughed. Celeste beamed. She couldn't help but feel proud of herself. Two days ago they hadn't even been speaking, and now they were not only speaking, they actually had inside jokes. This was how college was *supposed* to be.

"How about we write down the rules?" Jodi suggested. She

grabbed a yellow legal pad and a pen from her desk and wrote THE ALPHABETICAL HOOKUP LIST at the top of the page. "That way it'll all be official. We'll all be on the same page, so to speak."

Ali thought for a minute as she shoveled the stolen soup into her mouth. "I think we should discuss the prize first. I think it should be a great dinner out somewhere."

Jodi exchanged a quick glance with Celeste. "You have food on the brain, Ali," she said. "You better stop eating and start doing a lot more kissing."

"How about if the winner gets a night out on the town?" Celeste asked. It was the New Yorker in her talking. She really didn't even know why she was suggesting anything, considering there was no way she was going to win. But she was all caught up in the moment. Besides, on the way home tonight she'd checked out a book on narcissism from the Allween Library, and the checkout guy had been a very cute sophomore named Aaron who had horn-rimmed glasses and a V-necked argyle sweater. She'd promised herself to try to ask out Aaron-of-the-library tomorrow. Or soon. She just needed a little time to rebuild her self-esteem.

Ali was shaking her head. "I don't know, y'all. A night out in Athens, Georgia? What are we going to do—go to Dimers after a hot time peach-picking? I say we do a night in Atlanta. I know exactly where to go."

Hmmm, both Jodi and Celeste thought at the same time. Ali's idea of "exactly where to go" probably didn't coincide with theirs. It probably involved lollipops and glow sticks and a big warehouse-turned-rave with speakers blasting some deafening electronica. But they could worry about that later.

"Sounds good," Jodi said.

"Yeah," Celeste agreed. "And the winner gets to decide whatever we all do and the other two have to pay for everything."

Jodi nodded, even though she didn't have any money. But she just decided in her mind that there was no way she was going to lose. She started to record the rules:

1. *Each girl has to kiss (on the lips, and get kissed back, with tongue) one guy for every letter of the alphabet in order from A through Z for as long as it takes to think the alphabet song.*
2. *For each letter completed, each girl will receive a Scrabble tile with that letter on it.*
3. *If for some unfathomable reason the end of the school year comes and no one has completed their lists, the person with the most letters completed will be the winner.*
4. *The AHUL must be kept a secret.*[27]

"Anything else?" Jodi asked.

Celeste and Ali shook their heads. No one could think of any other rules.

27 The words *on pain of death* were crossed out after much deliberation.

"So when are we going to compare progress reports and dole out the Scrabble pieces?" Ali asked. She was excited. Winning this thing would be a piece of cake. And then she'd show Celeste and Jodi how to have a good time. A *real* good time.

"Let's have a meeting one week from today," Celeste said. That would give her a little time to at least get *A*.

"Okay," Jodi said. "Now we need a place to keep the rules."

"How about in the Scrabble game box?" Ali said.

"Too risky," Jodi said. "Someone from another room might borrow it and find it."

"Um . . . I have something we could use," Celeste mumbled. She sheepishly headed to the closet and pulled out a small bronze statue of a Buddha. His stomach was as wide and fat as he was tall—maybe twelve inches around. "Jib gave it to me. He got it in Hong Kong. It's a safe. You rub his stomach three times to the right and it opens."

Jodi gaped at it. "Oh my God," she mumbled. She'd never seen anything more tacky in her entire life.

Ali was equally appalled. "That's pretty unbelievable," she said.

Celeste rubbed his belly. Sure enough, the door popped open.

"You know, it's perfect," Jodi said. She solemnly folded the sheet of paper and placed it in the Buddha's stomach, as if she were performing a sacred rite. "No one will ever know."

"We'll meet one week from tonight," Ali said.

"I'll bring the Campbell's," Jodi offered.

Celeste took the Buddha from Jodi and kissed him

passionately on the lips. "Oh, Buddha, baby, you're a super-stah," she said in an English accent. "Hey, girls, I got my *B*."

Once again, to Celeste's immense delight, Jodi and Ali laughed.

"How are we supposed to wash these dishes?" Jodi said. "Can you wash dishes with shampoo?" She held up the bowl and pretended it was speaking. "Don't hate me because I'm beautiful. I use Pantene," the bowl said.

Jodi grabbed the three bowls and took them to the garbage room. Somebody had left a puke-stained T-shirt on the floor there. It was printed with the words *I'm With Stupid*.

For a moment Jodi felt another incredibly intense wave of sadness over her breakup with Buster. It hit her like that in waves during the day. How could they really be finished? Maybe he was just sowing his petty little oats, and soon he would get it out of his system. College *was* about experiment-ing, after all. But then she remembered the girl. She remem-bered those fake boobs. She remembered the look on Buster's face as he massaged them. And her stomach fell like their bowls down the garbage chute.

"Oh, Buster," she said out loud. His name echoed in the tiny garbage room in much the same way his fart had echoed in the Metropolitan Museum of Art. Okay. Enough. Pining wasn't going to get her anywhere. She had to stop this whole saying-his-name-out-loud thing. It was one thing to be dumped, but she didn't have to make herself all pathetic about it.

B was history. She had the whole rest of the alphabet ahead of her.

13

During the next week Jodi, Celeste, and Ali learned two very important and unpleasant things about college.[28] First of all, it wasn't true what they had always heard in high school—that you didn't have to go to class. If you didn't go to class, you were screwed. Second of all, you really had to study—at least, if you cared about doing well. But they did make one nice, collective discovery: The triple was actually not so heinous as they'd first imagined. It was almost an acceptable place to live—which was pretty amazing, considering that they still had no decorations on the walls, other than an abstract painting of Jib's and Ali's poster of Sasha & Digweed. In fact, all three of them found themselves looking forward to coming home at the end of each day. It was a refuge from the rest of the campus.

Jodi was having an extremely difficult time concentrating. For one thing, the mail room still hadn't found her fucking

28 Celeste didn't find these things as unpleasant as Jodi and Ali did.

boxes. But she could live with that. It was almost funny. (Well, not really.) The *real* problem was that every fifteen minutes or so, something totally random would remind her of Buster. She would see somebody wearing an If You Don't Like the Way I Drive, Get Off the Sidewalk T-shirt. She would see a guy with a bunch of golf clubs slung over his shoulder. Or worst of all, she'd see Buster himself—hobbling around on his crutches. No matter what she did, she couldn't stop thinking about him. She drifted through classes, signed up for track *and* soccer, rode a horse called Equinox a few times for the hell of it, and drank a lot of screwdrivers and coffee milk shakes in steady rotation. Nothing helped. Not even the Alphabetical Hookup List.

Ali wasn't faring any better. She spent most of the week in the Drop/Add office and at the animal shelter, walking the abandoned dogs and picking up their abandoned poop. Every time she tossed a little baggie of poop into the garbage, she would imagine that it was Sensei's soul. But then she would remember that he didn't have one.

Celeste was the only one who really became immersed in classes. In Psych 101 she was learning about Freud's theory of the Oedipus complex—namely, that every boy secretly wants to have sex with his mother and kill his father. In Modern Lit she was reading *Portnoy's Complaint,* by Philip Roth. It was about a neurotic Jewish man obsessed with sex. A lot of it was about masturbating. In Roman History she was studying the six vestal virgins of ancient Rome. The word *virgin* was said about a thousand times, and every time she heard it, Celeste turned bright red.

Sex, sex, sex. Celeste couldn't believe it. Every single college course was about sex in some way. She couldn't stop thinking about it. She was *required* to think about it. Unfortunately, her brain was the only part of her body that was getting any.

The following Sunday night at seven o'clock Jodi, Ali, and Celeste convened for their first weekly update. They had the supplies they needed to proceed: the Buddha, the drawstring bag of Scrabble pieces, paper, pencils, a bottle of tequila, a stolen saltshaker filled with stolen salt, and three PU shot glasses.

Ali poured the tequila into the shot glasses.

Celeste rubbed the Buddha's belly three times to the right.

Jodi removed the rule sheet from the secret chamber, unfolded it, and smoothed it out in front of them.

"Who goes first?" Jodi asked.

"Let's pick letters," Celeste said. "Whoever chooses the lowest letter goes first."

"Right on," Ali said. "*A* is low, *Z* is high."

They each reached into the bag of letters. Jodi turned her letter over: *A.* Ali chose *R,* and Celeste chose *S.*

Jodi grinned at the two of them. "Watch out, girls. I'm on a great streak. I'm already on *J.*" She took down her tequila shooter in one gulp to accentuate her statement.

Celeste gasped. "You're kidding!"

Ali downed her tequila and refilled both their glasses.

Jodi showed them the section of her Filofax labeled AHUL.

They all studied her list, poring over it with the same serious-ness and intensity the founding fathers must have exhibited when they examined the final draft of the Declaration of Independence.

ALPHABETICAL HOOKUP LIST

A: *Zit-faced Alex*
B: *Buster*
C: *Charlie*
D: *Druggie Steve + David Hasselhoff (I swear)*
E: *Eric*
F & G: *Gross Fredo*
H: *Jorge (pronounced Whore-hey) & Hot-dog Truck Steve*
I: *Ian*
J: *John (and Jorge)*

Ali and Celeste frowned at each other.

Jodi was still grinning. She gulped down the next shot of tequila. "What?" she said.

"What the hell is this?" Ali demanded.

Jodi blinked. "It's my list. *A* through *J.*"

"I don't think so." Celeste shook her head vehemently. She sipped at her tequila. The taste made her grimace.

"I'm sorry, but you've got some serious explaining to do," Ali said.

"What are you talking about?" Jodi asked, suddenly feeling guilty and defensive. "Alex and Buster and Charlie are pretty self-explanatory. Agreed?"

Celeste raised her eyebrows. "Well, I don't know if Buster should count. How hard is it to hook up with someone you've hooked up with for six years? And you're not even supposed to be seeing him, let alone kissing him. You promised us you wouldn't call him."

"I didn't call him," Jodi said. "I ran into him, kissed him, and then slapped him really hard across the face."

Ali and Celeste both smiled. "Really?" they asked at the same time.

Jodi nodded. The three of them laughed. Celeste poured some more tequila. It really wasn't so bad, once you got used to the burning in your throat and intestines.

"Okay, that counts," Ali conceded. "Since you slapped him. That's pretty cool. But *here's* where our problem begins." She pointed to the *D* entry. "Druggie Steve? David Hasselhoff?"

Jodi shrugged. "Well, Steve *is* a druggie. In fact, I think he deals. I could have called him Dealer Steve. And then there was this guy talking on a pay phone in town, and I swear if it wasn't David Hasselhoff, then it was his look-alike."

"So, it wasn't in fact David Hasselhoff," Celeste said.

"I think it was," Jodi said. "Although David Hasselhoff's kind of tall, right? This guy was pretty short. Maybe he just looks tall in the movies."

Ali smirked. "So that's out. And what is this *F* and *G*? Dude, one guy can't count for two letters!"

"And *H* is a scam, too," Celeste chimed in. "Jorge is a *J*—and Hot-dog Truck Steve? First of all, *eeew,* and second, he's an *S.*"

"The letter *I* looks legit, I guess," Ali said, her eyes narrowing.

"Oh my God, it was great," Jodi said. She started smiling again. The shots were going straight to her head. "We met at a Kappa Kappa Gamma party. I got there late because of kitchen duty, and he was the very first person I saw when I opened the door. He was like, 'Hey, beautiful, what's your name—I'm Ian.' And I was like, 'Good. I need an *I*.' I just grabbed him and started making out with him."

"Well, that definitely counts," Ali said.

"And who's John?" Celeste said, feeling a little jealous. She couldn't help it. She was filled with envy and embarrassment and pangs of worthlessness. She hadn't kissed anybody yet. At all. It was so pitiful.

"Well . . . ," Jodi said.

"Well, what?" Ali and Celeste said together.

"Well," Jodi explained, "it was at the same party. I guess I was a little wasted. I walked up to this really cute guy, and I was like, 'Your name doesn't happen to start with *J*, does it?' And he was like, 'My name can start with whatever you want it to start with.' So I said, 'Well, what's your name, then?' and he was like, 'Well, how about we say my name is John, would you like that?' I was like, 'Sounds good, John.' And then we made out."

Ali and Celeste exchanged another frown.

Jodi blushed slightly, but that might have just been the tequila.

"Okay, so this list is, like, totally bogus," Ali said, as diplomatically as possible.

"Nicknames can't count," Celeste said.

"If nicknames don't count, then Buster doesn't count," Jodi said. She paused for a minute, wondering if she should divulge Buster's biggest secret. "His real name is Melvin." She finished up her third shot. "Melvin Needham."

"Melvin!" Ali and Celeste shrieked at the same time.

"I know, I know." Jodi groaned. "Look, I think a nickname should count if it's the name that everybody knows the person by."

Ali nodded. "That's fair. But it can't be a new nickname you give them, like 'Hot-dog Truck Steve.' I mean, does anybody but you really call this guy Fredo 'Gross Fredo'?"

"Well, no. But *A, B,* and *C* count. And Eric counts. He's just some boring-ass guy named Eric who I can barely remember kissing."

"All right, so you have *A, B, C,* and *E,*" Celeste said. "But we're supposed to do them in order. So you really only have *A, B,* and *C.*"

"You know, y'all, I was actually thinking of an exception to that rule," Ali said. "I think we should be able to get a letter out of order if we go all the way with the person. That should be the only exception to the hooking-up-in-order rule."

Jodi nodded. "I agree," she said.

"Okay, fine," Celeste mumbled. *Not that it would make any difference in my case,* she thought.

Jodi wrote two more amendments to the official list of rules.

5. A nickname has to be universally known and accepted, e.g., Buster.

6. You can add a name to your list out of order only if you sleep with the guy.

"Okay, my turn," Ali said confidently. She was already on J, too, but her list was real. And she hadn't even tried. Not that hard, anyway.

> *The Alphabetical Thingy Game*
> A: *Amelia*
> B: *Barbara*
> C: *Chris*
> D: *Diane*
> E: *Eve*
> F: *Frieda*
> G: *Guinevere*
> H: *Hallie Tosis*
> I: *Ian*
> J: *Jennifer*

Celeste's jaw was the first to drop. Jodi's jaw wasn't far behind. They gaped at each other. *Amelia? Barbara? Diane? Eve?* There were only two men on the whole list: Chris and Ian. And Hallie Tosis—*oh my God.*

"And you thought *my* list was bad?" Jodi shouted. She started giggling. "This is so bogus! At least I managed to kiss members of the opposite sex."

Ali shrugged. "What? I kissed all those dudes. In order, too."

"That's precisely the problem," Jodi said. "They're not *dudes.*"

"I don't see what's so wrong with it," Ali said.

"There's only two men on this list," Celeste said.

"Wait a minute, I'm not even so sure about that," Jodi said. Her eyes scanned the paper again. "Chris? Is he a boy or a girl?"

"Well, he's a girl," Ali admitted. "But he's very butch."

"Then it doesn't count!" Jodi practically screamed.

"You really kissed all these girls?" Celeste asked, feeling her face get hot.

"Sweetie, you're way too inhibited," Ali muttered. "Why do we have to label everything? It's college, y'all. Love is where you find it."

"But Hallie Tosis?" Jodi asked. "Hallie Tosis? *Hallie Tosis?*"

"I know, that was pretty bad," Ali said. "But I needed an *H,* and she was there."

"Were you a 'superstah'?" Celeste joked in a breathy voice. She took another sip of tequila.

Ali laughed, even though she was a little annoyed. "I'm sure I was. You know, Celeste, that's not a fine French wine. It's tequila. I never saw anyone sip tequila." She and Jodi both downed another shot. Celeste squeezed her eyes shut and did the same.

Jodi wrote the next rule in extra-large capital letters.

7. MEMBERS OF THE OPPOSITE SEX ONLY!!!

"Fine," Ali said. "Whatever. But I get to keep Ian because I slept with him. That's the rule we just agreed to."

"Uh, what was Ian's last name?" Jodi asked. "Just out of curiosity."

"Haas," Ali said.

Jodi felt a fresh wave of depression. "Red hair, green eyes?"

"I don't really remember his eyes, to tell you the truth—but yeah, he definitely had red hair," Ali said. "Really curly, too."

Jodi hung her head. It was the same Ian, all right. Of course, she knew she shouldn't be mad at Ali—or even sad for herself. It wasn't as if she cared about this Ian. She didn't even know Ian's last name. Still, after having been in love with the same guy for six years, this whole thing was all just a little . . . *sordid.* She quickly poured her fourth shot. Or was it her fifth?

"Well, you get to keep Ian," Celeste said.

"And I should get to keep Chris," Ali insisted. "She looks like a man."

Celeste and Jodi were so grossed out that they almost agreed, just to change the subject. But the rules were the rules.

"How far did you go with her—him?" Jodi asked bravely.

"Just a kiss," Ali said.

"Then it doesn't count, because it wasn't in order," Celeste said.

Jodi sifted through the Scrabble pieces and took an *A, B, C,* for herself. She handed an *I* to Ali.

"When did you have sex with Ian Haas?" Jodi asked.

"Wednesday,"[29] Ali said.

Jodi pursed her lips. "Ugh, what a dog," she said. "That's when I kissed him."

Ali shrugged. "Guys are guys, y'all. They're all dogs. What can I say? Now do you see why I prefer kissing women?" She turned to Celeste. "Okay, it's your turn."

Celeste bit her lip. This was so humiliating. She felt like jumping up and bolting from the room. "Well, for one thing, I played the game honestly," she muttered, staring hard at the bottle of tequila to avoid looking either Jodi or Ali in the eye. "If I had tried to cheat like you guys, I would have gotten to *Z.*"

"Celeste," Jodi said gently. She had a feeling Celeste hadn't gotten too far. It was hard, though. Harder than Jodi had thought it would be, for sure—even with her foolproof strategy. And poor Celeste was repressed with a capital *R.*

"How many did you get?" Ali asked.

Celeste took a deep breath. There wasn't any point in pro-longing the agony. She opened her notebook.

The College Men of Celeste Alexander (in Alphabetical Order)
   A:

"Happy now?" she grumbled.

□□□□□□□□□□□□□□□□□□□□□□□□□□□

29 Everyone knows Wednesday is the new Thursday.

Ali's face softened. She shot a quick glance at Jodi, then patted Celeste on the shoulder. "Don't worry about it, Celeste. It's only the first week of school."

"You'll catch up with us in no time," Jodi added.

Celeste glanced up at them. "Do you really think so?" she asked.

"Definitely," Ali said. "Dude, it's only been one week."

"The year has just begun," Jodi said.

"It just takes one to break the ice," Ali said.

"Totally," Jodi said. "Once you kiss your first one, guys will be falling out of the trees."

Celeste smiled. It was funny to think of boys falling out of trees.

"We'll probably be taking *you* out in Atlanta," Ali said.

All at once Celeste was blushing again. She felt like kissing *them.* "Thanks, guys," she murmured.

"Not that I'm saying this is going to happen, but if you die a virgin, it would be okay because you'd become a saint," Ali said. *Whoops.* As soon as she'd finished, she wondered if maybe she should have kept her mouth shut. But she was sort of tipsy.

"Not a saint, an angel," Celeste said.

"I think it would be cool to be a saint." Ali stood and strolled over to Celeste's bookshelf, weaving slightly. She pulled out the biography of Saint Lucia. "What is this dude the saint of?"

"Put that back," Celeste said nervously. "She's the saint of eyesight. I prayed to her when I was a child that I wouldn't have to get glasses, but I did, anyway."

Ali opened the book. Her eyes bulged. There was a color print of an Asian man and woman doing a sixty-nine. "Whoa! Saint Lucia is definitely my kind of saint. Hey, what is this? This isn't about a saint. This is about kinky sex!" She peeled off the Saint Lucia cover and exposed the *Kama Sutra.* Then she beamed at Celeste. "Dude!" she cried.

"Dude!" Jodi said, laughing.

Celeste's cheeks were flaming, but she downed her shot. "See, girls, there's more to me than meets the eye."

"I guess so," Ali said.

They got into their beds and Ali read the *Kama Sutra* aloud until they all passed out.

14

The next evening, without warning or explanation, a representative of PU appeared at the door of the triple with an answering machine. Needless to say, Jodi's stuff was still nowhere to be found. Still, the answering machine was nothing short of a miracle. Whoever was the saint of phones had finally come through for them. Hallelujah!

Ali plugged it in. The three of them spent twenty minutes recording their outgoing message, running through about fifty takes before they all agreed that they got it right. They decided to keep it simple (so as not to sound desperate) but also to make it seem like they were having the time of their lives—just in case Buster, Sensei, or Jordan called.

As soon as they were finished, the phone rang. They stared at it.

"Who's going to answer?" Celeste said.

"Not me!" Jodi said.

"Let's test our message out," Ali said.

The machine picked up after the third ring.

"What's up, people?" the voices of Ali, Jodi, and Celeste asked in unison. "Gin & Juice," by Snoop Dogg and Dr. Dre, played quietly in the background. "We're out and about. Please leave a message."

They looked at each other and nodded. Perfect.

Beep!

"Hi, Jodi, this is Fredo . . . you know, from the kitchen. Hey. Okay. [Nervous, high-pitched giggle.] You know, I was really psyched on that kiss you gave me in the kitchen, and you really didn't have to run away like that. I was wondering if you want to do something this weekend. There's a WWF match we could go to. Anyway, I'll see you later tonight. Okay, bye."

Click.

Celeste and Ali burst out laughing. *The WWF?* Good Lord.

"Oh my God," Jodi said. She felt sick. She'd forgotten there might actually be some ramifications to kissing these guys.

The phone rang again.

Jodi grabbed it, determined to nip this whole Gross Fredo thing in the bud. "Hello?"

"Um . . . yeah. Hi. Is Celeste there, please?"

It wasn't Gross Fredo. But it *was* a guy. Jodi grinned. "Sure. Can I ask who's calling?"

"Um . . . Andy. From her psych class."

Jodi handed the phone to Celeste. "It's for you." She winked. "It's someone named Andy. And we all know what letter *Andy* starts with."

Ali flashed Celeste a thumbs-up.

It looked like Celeste's luck was finally changing. She had a gentleman caller, as they said in Georgia. True, it was Andy the Bloated, but still. . . .

"Hello?" she asked.

"Hi. Celeste?"

"Yes?"

"Um . . . I was just wondering. Do you have any interest in seeing *Gone with the Wind* at the two-dollar revival house this Saturday night?"

Celeste didn't ask him what had happened to his girlfriend, mostly because she didn't really care. Besides, if Ali could kiss Hallie Tosis, then she could kiss Andy the Bloated, no questions asked. "Sure," she told him. "But isn't that like four hours long?"

Andy the Bloated laughed nervously. "Well, yeah, but every second is worth it. You'll see. Plus, um, they have intermission. You'll love it. Really. It's my favorite—" He started sneezing.

"Okay," Celeste said. Beggars couldn't be choosers. It was a date, and it was a date with an *A*—even if it meant sitting next to Andy the Bloated for four hours. "I'll meet you there."

"Great!"

Just as she was about to hang up, the call waiting went off. She clicked the button.

"Hello?" she asked.

"Jodi!" a gruff voice barked.

"No, this is Celeste."

"I *know*. I want to speak to Jodi."

Celeste frowned. "Oh." She shrugged and handed the phone back to Jodi. "For you."

"Not again," Jodi muttered. She rolled her eyes. "Look, Fredo, I know I kissed you and everything, but—"

"Who's Fredo?"

Jodi gasped. Her face went white. It was *Buster*. "I . . . uh . . ."

"Who's Fredo?" Buster repeated.

All of a sudden Jodi found that she was enraged. "It's none of your fucking business who Fredo is," she snapped. "Why are you calling me?"

Silence.

"Well? Hello? Buster?"

Celeste and Ali were staring at her. She turned away from them.

"Look, Jo . . . I . . . I feel terrible," Buster murmured. "I miss you so much. I'm so sorry. It's over between me and Cathi, and it never meant—"

"Cathi? Her name is Mandi!"

Buster sniffed. "Well, it's over with both of them. You know you're the only one for me. We're Buster and Jodi, together forever. Remember?"

Jodi didn't answer. She didn't know whether she wanted to burst into tears or slam the phone down on the hook or start screaming . . . or all of the above.

"Remember?" Buster prodded.

"What I remember is that you were pawing some bimbo's boobs in a frat house bathroom," Jodi growled.

"I said I was sorry. Can't we at least get together and talk?"

Jodi didn't know what else to say. Especially with Ali and Celeste right there in the room.

"I was thinking," Buster continued, "that we could maybe go to a movie—some kind of chick flick you would like—and then we could really talk all this through."

Jodi's throat tightened. "I don't know," she said. "Look, Buster, it's late. I really have to be getting to the dining hall—"

"I know you're angry, and I don't blame you," Buster gently interrupted. "I'm just asking you to think about it."

"Fine," Jodi said. "I'll think about it."

"Okay, great!"

"Bye." Jodi hung up. She rolled her eyes at her room-mates, then shook her head and stalked out of the room. She had to go to work. But she wasn't sure if she had done the right thing. It was true, a part of her belonged to Buster. But no matter how many times he said he was sorry, the facts remained: After only a week of college, he had already cheated on her. At least once. Who knew how many more times he had cheated behind her back? No, she had to move on. Right. Buster was part of her childhood. It was time to start being an adult.

By the time Jodi reached the kitchen, she had changed her mind.

Buster wasn't just her high school sweetheart. He was a huge part of her whole *life.* Not to mention the fact that unless one of them transferred, they had to go to the same college for the next four years. So what would be the harm in going to see a movie with him? On the other hand, why should she give him the time of day?

Man. She really needed to talk about this with somebody. But she couldn't talk about it with her roommates, because it was obvious that they hated Buster. They *were* good listeners, though. And very understanding about boy problems. Still, with the creation of the Alphabetical Hookup List, they'd all sort of made a pact to leave the past behind and move on. So maybe she could talk to . . . no, that was crazy. She shook her head as she grabbed her apron and hair net off one of the hooks near the kitchen door. She'd actually thought, *Maybe I could talk to Zack about this.* He was smart, after all. And he was a guy. So maybe he'd have some insight. Some perspective. At the very least, he could make her laugh. She smiled, thinking of how he'd stolen the giant watermelon. What a freak.

"Hi, Jodi!"

Jodi groaned. It was Gross Fredo. She turned and saw him by the deep-fat fryer. He made a smooching face with his lips pursed at her.

"Is Zack here?" she demanded.

Gross Fredo looked hurt. "No. Hey, did you get my message about—"

"Where is he, then?" Jodi asked.

"You didn't hear?" Gross Fredo said with a sneer. "He was fired. Can you imagine getting fired from this place? Lips hasn't fired anyone in over ten years. As the Sinatra song goes, if you can't make it here, you can't make it anywhere."

Jodi's eyes narrowed. "Why was he fired?"

"Look out the window."

She glanced through the glass out at the lawn. There was a corny statue of Stonewall Jackson right outside the dining hall—with his head turned behind him and his sword waving in the air, as if he were leading a charge. Only this evening, something about him was different. In the fading light of the setting sun Jodi could see that he was covered in pink droplets and tiny black seeds. A destroyed watermelon rind lay at his feet like the head of the Yankee enemy.

"You!"

Jodi whirled around to find herself facing the wrath of Lips.

"You!" he barked again, waving his magic spoon. "You knew about this."

"No, I didn't," Jodi protested, shaking her head.

"You were probably up there on the roof with that hairy animal."

"No, I swear, I didn't know anything about it until just now—"

"If you value your job, you will go out there and wash that thing right now," Lips interrupted. He thrust his spoon toward a bucket and washcloth in the corner. The bucket was full of grimy, sudsy water. "I will not have my employees throwing things from the roof! Now get to work. There's a ladder at the bottom of the stairwell."

Jodi opened her mouth, then closed it. Whatever. Washing Stonewall Jackson was better than slaving over a grill full of grade-F burgers with Gross Fredo. She grabbed the bucket and headed outside.

For the rest of the evening Jodi scrubbed the bronze statue, or "Stoney," as she began to call him. She worked her way from bottom to top, up and up the ladder. By the time she reached his neck, it was almost nine o'clock. When she got to his face, she kissed him, wondering if that would earn her an *S.* There was no rule in the AHUL saying that the guy couldn't be made out of bronze. She laughed to herself. College was nothing at all like she'd thought it would be.

What would Daddy think now, she wondered, *if he could see me swabbing down Confederate General Stonewall Jackson's crotch area?* Maybe the problem was that she was a Yankee. That was probably why things weren't going well for her here in the South. She flicked a watermelon seed from between Stonewall's legs.

Suddenly she noticed that a shadowy male figure was staring at her from near the dining hall door. She peered at him.

"Holy shit," the figure said.

Jodi smiled. It was Zack. She hadn't even recognized him. For once, his hair seemed fairly tame. It actually wasn't so bad looking when it wasn't sticking out in a zillion different directions.

"Stalking me?" she asked.

"No, no. Hey, Jodi, I am so sorry," he apologized. He tiptoed toward her, glancing in each direction. His eyelids were so heavy that he looked like he was about to fall asleep. "I never thought they'd make *you* clean it up."

"Don't worry about it," Jodi said with a shrug. "I'm sort of enjoying it."

Zack laughed. "Yeah, I can see that."

"Stoney and I have a special relationship," Jodi said. She wrapped her arm around his bronze waist. "An unspoken bond."

"Well, you're certainly making the old guy happy. I think I almost caught him smiling."

"I guess I have the magic touch," she said.

Zack bit his lip. "Hey, look, I do feel bad. I want to do something to make it up to you."

Jodi stared at him. "Like what?"

"I don't know. I'll think about it. Maybe I'll take you somewhere or something." He lit up a cigarillo, smiled at her, then turned and wandered back into the night. "I'll see ya around," he called over his shoulder.

"Yeah, see ya around," Jodi said.

She watched him go. His hair rustled in the night breeze. Then she frowned. *Wait a second.* Had Zack just asked her out on a date? Or sort of, anyway? No . . . that was impossible. Then again, weirder things had happened. All she had to do was glance up at the smiling face of Stoney to be reminded of that.

15

The thing was, lesbianism just wasn't for Ali. She had given it the good old "college try," but it just wasn't working out for her the way she had hoped. Maybe she just wasn't same-sex oriented. First of all, the members of the Lesbian Alliance were way too serious. They never joked around, and they especially hated gay jokes. And they didn't seem to want to have any real fun. No dancing. No drinking. Just sitting around and moping. It was a serious bummer. Her whole *life* was a serious bummer—except for her roommates, which somehow made life even *more* of a bummer.

She was even thinking about giving up the animal shelter. How was she supposed to go to classes, hook up with twenty-six guys (well, twenty-four guys now), and hold down a volunteer job? Still . . . being around animals all the time made her think about becoming a vet. And she was learning a lot from Ed—or Nice Ed, as she called him, because with his skinny frame and tousled brown hair he was much nicer than he was cute (but not *un*-cute) —a twenty-two-year-old vet in training there. Hey, *E!* She had gotten both *A* (Antonio) and *B* (Brian) that morning in biology. Too bad she had no idea what was actually going on in class. Oh, well. Even if she flunked biology, she was still good with animals. A lot better with animals than she was with people, it seemed.

Usually, anyway.

Right now she wasn't feeling very good with either people *or* animals. She'd been walking an enormous black-and-white Great Dane named Shorty for almost an hour now, and he still hadn't gone. And it was getting late. Her shift ended at ten.

"Come on, go already," she pleaded.

Finally he squatted down. A tiny little turd fell onto the sidewalk. Ali fished a little baggie from her jeans pocket and picked up the poop, using the bag as a glove. She scanned the street for a nearby garbage can. None was in sight.

"Don't you *hate* when that happens?" a voice called behind her.

She looked up. Nice Ed was strolling toward her. He looked a lot cuter at night. Especially in that white lab coat. It seemed to fill him out a little bit.

"Ha ha, very funny," Ali said. Okay, not the most brilliant comeback of all time.

Ed patted Shorty on the head. "Hi, cutie," he said. "There's a garbage can around the corner."

"Are you talking to me or to him?" Ali asked flirtatiously.

"I'm talking to the one of you who's not holding the bag of

dog shit," Ed said, smiling. "You know, Ali, that's not exactly the biggest turn-on in the world."

Ali smiled back. "I guess you're right."

"Come on, follow me," Nice Ed said. "We have a new guest at the shelter."

"Uh, just let me get rid of this," she said. She ran down the street to the garbage can around the corner, wondering if Ed was looking at her ass. She sort of had a feeling that he was.

"Okay, ready?" he asked.

Ali and Shorty followed Ed inside. Ed led Ali down a long, narrow hall to their boss's office. For a second Ali wondered if Nice Ed was going to make a move on her. Their boss, a three-hundred-pound man named Dr. Woo, had long since gone home. His office door was closed. Ed paused outside it. His zits looked a lot worse under the fluorescent lights.

"All right," he whispered. "I'm gonna show you something. But promise you won't tell anyone."

"Sure," Ali said. She couldn't help but feel a little nervous.

Ed opened the door. Ali's jaw dropped.

A chimpanzee was sitting in their boss's desk chair. He was wearing overalls and holding a framed picture of their boss's wife. He was kissing the picture with his big, puckered, chimpanzee lips.

"Oh my God!" Ali breathed.

"Hey, Kid," Ed said.

The chimp put the picture back on the desk, got up from the chair, and waddled over to them. He jumped into Ali's arms and wrapped his own arms around her neck.

"Well, hello, dude!" she exclaimed delightedly. He was actually pretty heavy. She grunted under his weight.

"I knew you two would get along," Ed said. "But remember: Don't tell anyone. We're not really supposed to have him here. His name is Kid Charlemagne. You might have seen him at the zoo. A friend of mine who works there set him free. I'm just figuring out what's the best thing to do with him."

Ali nodded, staring into Kid's wandering brown eyes. Wow. Ed was pretty hard-core. Ali did love animals, but she didn't exactly spend all her time at the zoo memorizing all of their names and everything. She had a life that actually involved some *people.* Or she wanted to have one, anyway.

"I won't say anything," Ali promised.

"All right, well, I'll leave you two alone for a few minutes to get better acquainted," Ed said. He closed the door behind him. Kid Charlemagne jumped down from Ali's arms and crawled over to the filing cabinet. He opened the bottom drawer and pulled out a big bottle of bourbon. Ali laughed. Man, having a chimp would be so cool. Maybe she could take him home for just one night so he could meet Jodi and Celeste.

Or maybe . . .

A smile spread across her face. Nah.

But then again, why not?

The rule was you had to kiss someone of the opposite sex. And Kid Charlemagne was most definitely male. The rules didn't mention anything about human males, and besides, man had evolved from apes, and Kid Charlemagne was less apelike than most of the guys on campus. He was definitely less of an ape than Buster. And she was up to *C.* Kid Charlemagne should actually count for *K,* too, since it was a really hard letter. So what if . . . oh, what the hell. Why not?

She poured herself a glass of bourbon. Then she poured a little splash of bourbon into the Kid's baby bottle, screwed the nipple back on, and gave it to him.

"I'd like to propose a toast, dude," she said. "To us."

She held up her glass. The Kid held up his baby bottle. They drank in unison.

16

"I hope you know that I really want us to get back together," Buster said to Jodi in a loud voice just as the lights in the theater dimmed. "I mean, I must want to get back together if I agreed to see a lame movie like this."

"Shhh!" Jodi hissed crossly. "*Gone with the Wind* is a classic. And it's all about Georgia."

"So's that TV show *Designing Women*, but that doesn't mean I want to watch it."

Jodi smiled, and instantly hated herself for it. It was so typical: Buster was joking around and making *her* feel guilty—even though he'd suggested they see a "chick flick" and he was entirely to blame for their breakup. She kept her eyes fixed on the screen, even though she wasn't paying any attention. Somebody in the front of the theater sneezed very loudly. Then he sneezed again. "You've liked a lot of the movies I've taken you to," she muttered.

"No, I haven't," Buster said. "Name one."

"*Billy Elliot.* That movie about the little boy ballerina, remember?"

"Shut up!" Buster whispered. He propped himself up in his seat and glanced around the theater. His crutches fell to the floor with a loud *crack.* "I might know someone here. I knew you were going to bring that up."

Jodi allowed herself a little chuckle. "As I seem to recall, you also loved *Stepmom.*"

"Will you two pipe down?" somebody behind them hissed.

Buster sank back down in the cushions. "All right, all right," he muttered. "I'll give this a try, but just don't tell anyone about those other two, okay? Like I said, I want to make this work. I'm sorry. And anyway, I already paid my two bucks."

Jodi nodded, satisfied.

"You know, the light from a black-and-white screen makes you look really cute," he breathed in her ear. He leaned close to her.

"Thank you," Jodi said curtly. She resisted an urge to hold Buster's hand. She had to be careful. She didn't just want them to fall into their old patterns without really thinking and talking about it first. It was amazing how comfortable she felt with him, though. How many times had they sat together like this? How many movies had they seen? Yes, Buster had made a mistake. A terrible, disgusting, foul, grotesque mistake. But college was hard for everyone. Maybe he deserved a second chance. After all, she'd kissed Gross Fredo. Not that Buster had to know anything about that—or anything about the Alphabetical Hookup List at all. No. Part of being an adult was having the good sense *not* to share certain things.

She slowly inched her hand toward him and let it slip onto his knee. She felt his big hand wrap around hers the way it had thousands of times before. His cast was stuck out into the aisle. It was an old-fashioned movie theater, with curtains and art deco lights and nice big cushioned seats. This was fun. She was glad Celeste had lent her a nice plaid dress to wear. She was still wearing sneakers, though, because her feet were bigger than her roommates'. Not that it mattered. Buster, she noticed, hadn't exactly dressed up. He was wearing jeans and his Chicks Dig Me T-shirt. But of course, Jodi had given that one to him.

On the screen Mammy was lacing Scarlett O'Hara into her corset.

"You know, this would actually be kind of a hot scene if Mammy was a hot young chick," Buster whispered.

Jodi shook her head. She withdrew her hand from his. "Wow, that's really insightful," she snapped. "Have you ever thought about being a professional film critic?"

Buster laughed. "I'm just saying it has potential. You know, two hot chicks and a corset. This scene should also have a spanking. Yeah. That fat one should get a really *big* spanking for being such a naughty porker."

"Will you stop it?" Jodi snapped. She knew he was being deliberately gross just to make her laugh. But now was definitely *not* the time. In fact, she wasn't just annoyed. She was pissed. "*Gone with the Wind* is not a porno movie."

"Well, it should be," Buster grumbled. "Anyway, I'm just trying to enjoy myself." Someone in the front of the theater kept sneezing.

"That's really annoying the shit out of me," Buster said.

"Just ignore it," Jodi said.

They listened to about five more sneezes.

"Hey, this is a movie theater, not a fucking hospital," Buster shouted.

A few people in the theater laughed.

"SHUT UP!" somebody shouted at them.

"BLOW ME!" Buster shouted back.

More laughter.

"Enough," Jodi whispered, hitting his arm. This time, though, she giggled. One of the things she loved most about Buster was his ability to make fun of someone's being a moron—when he, in fact, was a moron himself. He was a genius that way.

Buster took her hand again.

Jodi sighed. She'd already missed the first five minutes of the movie, and there was no way she could concentrate. Her mind wandered to the Kappa Kappa Gamma pledge party later that night. It was the famous annual *Gone with the Wind* theme party—the one they always held right before they picked their freshman pledges. All pledges had to go as their favorite character. One of the reasons she'd wanted to come to this movie—the main reason, really, aside from reconciling with Buster—was so she could get ideas for a costume.

The *Gone with the Wind* party was the most important pledge party of the year. Way more important than Alice in Gammaland. Her stupid job was ruining everything. She had to get a great costume together, but she couldn't think of anything in Celeste's wardrobe that would work. Ali's wardrobe was out of the question. Jodi scanned the seats, looking for Celeste. She thought Celeste was supposed to be there with Andy the Bloated, but she couldn't see where they were. Poor Celeste. She was just supposed to kiss the guy. She didn't have to go out on a whole date with him. Jodi wished she could have a little powwow with Celeste in the ladies' room for a minute, just to talk about her costume. . . .

There she is.

Celeste had stood. She was rushing past them up the aisle.

"I have to go to the ladies' room," Jodi whispered to Buster. She climbed over him and his big leg and followed Celeste out into the lobby.

"Hey," Jodi said.

Celeste didn't look very happy. "Oh, hey," she mumbled.

"What's wrong?" Jodi asked.

"I don't think this is going very well," Celeste said. "Andy keeps sneezing because of his allergies and some jerk yelled that the theater isn't a fucking hospital and everybody laughed. Andy got really embarrassed. Now he's all pouty, and he ran out of Kleenexes. I told him I'd run to the bathroom and get him some, but that was just because he was getting on my nerves."

Jodi flashed an awkward smile. She chose not to tell Celeste that the jerk was Buster. "I'm sorry, Celeste. Hey, do you have any ideas for what I could wear to the *Gone with the Wind* party tonight? You don't happen to have a hoop skirt? Oh my God, why did I wait this long?"

Celeste thought for a minute. "I have a blue velvet dress with velvet buttons," she said.

"Hmmm," Jodi said. She didn't want to seem unappreciative, but on the other hand, she didn't want to go as Bonnie Blue Butler.

"I bet everyone's going to go as Scarlett," Celeste said. "You should go as Melanie. She's the best character. Just wear something drab."

Jodi laughed. "No, she's not the best character! She's such a namby-pamby. But you're right, everyone will be dressed as Scarlett."

"Why don't you go as Belle Watkins?" Celeste suggested.

"The hooker?"

"Why not? She's a great character, and you'll probably be the only one."

"Maybe," Jodi said, "and I think I just had a great idea."

"What is it?" Celeste asked.

"I'll show you later," Jodi said. "I better get to work on it. Good luck with Andy."

"Thanks," Celeste said. "We need it."

When Jodi got back to her seat, she found Buster pouring rum into his jumbo soda cup. "Rum and Sprite," he whispered. "It's so awesome. Want some?"

Jodi scowled at him as she sat down. "No, thanks. Uh . . .

hey, Buster? Weren't we supposed to talk about our relationship after this?"

On the screen Scarlett threw something across the room.

Buster shrugged. "Yeah? So?"

"So, why are you drinking—"

"I'm starting to get into this," Buster interrupted, his eyes glued to the movie. "Miss Scarlett's a feisty one. And a hot one." He slurped down half the cup in one huge gulp, then burped. "Ahhh. I gotta take a leak."

"Thanks for sharing," Jodi grumbled. She caught a whiff of his breath. It stank.

"But it's just starting to get good," Buster whined. "I have a feeling Scarlett's gonna show some titty soon."

Jodi's face shriveled in disgust. Was it her imagination, or was he being even more of a pig than usual? Weren't they trying to patch things up? Wasn't that the whole point of coming to this stupid movie in the first place—when she should have been worrying about her costume for the Kappa Kappa Gamma pledge party?

"Well, I think something good's going to happen and I'm not going to miss it," Buster said. He unzipped his pants.

"Wha-what are you doing?" Jodi stammered.

"I gotta take a piss."

"Well, then wait until the intermission—"

"I can't wait," Buster said.

To Jodi's utter horror, Buster whipped out his dick and pissed long and hard into the jumbo soda cup. When he finished, he put the lid back on the cup and the straw back in the hole in the lid. Then he smiled and put the cup down on the floor between them.

All right. This was too much. Jodi couldn't believe he would do something *this* gross. She was totally repulsed. She wasn't even heartbroken anymore. She just knew she wanted to be as far away as possible from this . . . this . . . this *child*. Yes. This was it. They were through. It was over. For good. She was not going to marry a man who pissed in a cup in a movie theater for fear of missing some "titty." During *Gone with the Wind,* for Christ's sake.

"What?" Buster asked.

Jodi stood up and stormed out. And frankly, my dear, she didn't give a damn.

Celeste wasn't having much better luck with Andy the Bloated. He was even more nervous than she was. He couldn't stop fidgeting and sneezing.

"Achoo."

"Bless you."

"Sorry."

"Don't be sorry."

"Achoo."

"Bless you."

"Sorry."

"Don't be sorry."

"Achoo . . ."

It was an endless loop.

She knew she just had to kiss him and get it over with.

There was no point in prolonging the torture. For either of them. This was absolutely the worst date ever. But she had to at least earn her *A*. She couldn't imagine suffering through this evening and not at least getting an *A* out of it. But Andy the Bloated wasn't making any move whatsoever. He was just sitting there, blowing his nose into the toilet paper she'd brought him.

He tried to turn to smile at her. His nose was runny.

Celeste couldn't stand it anymore. She grabbed Andy the Bloated and kissed him just as Rhett Butler had kissed Scarlett O'Hara. Only it wasn't exactly the same as Rhett and Scarlett. Because Andy the Bloated farted. *During* the kiss. There was no doubt about it. Celeste heard the fart, loud and clear. So did half the theater.

Andy the Bloated was horrified. "Oh God, I'm sorry."

Celeste just shook her head. She was horrified, too.

"Gross!" someone behind them yelled.

"Please be gone, nobody wants to smell your wind," someone else yelled.

A lot of people started laughing.

"Gone with the wind!" the first guy yelled. "Gone with the wind!"

The chant swept through the theater. Soon everybody else was joining in: *"Gone with the wind! Gone with the wind! Gone with the . . ."*

Then Andy the Bloated started sneezing again. Violently.

"Are you okay?" Celeste whispered. She was starting to get scared. He looked like he was having a seizure or something. He didn't answer. Finally he managed to stagger to his feet. "I'm leaving," he choked out. "Too much dust . . ."

"Do you want me to go with you?" Celeste asked.

"No, please stay," Andy the Bloated managed. She heard his sneezes moving up the aisle and then fading into the lobby.

Some people applauded.

"What a loser," someone commented.

Celeste sank down in her seat. Yes, that was true. But there was another loser equally as lame in this theater, and her name was Celeste Alexander. She buried her face in her hands. She'd wait until intermission and then leave, too.

When the word *Intermission* finally appeared on the screen, Celeste jumped up from her seat and headed up the aisle. She froze about halfway to the exit. Buster was sitting there, crying. Tears were streaming down his face. He looked like a little boy.

"Hey, are you all right?" Celeste asked. "Where's Jodi?"

"She left," he sobbed. "We're really through this time."

"I'm sorry," Celeste said.

Buster sniffed and glanced up at her. "Me too," he said. He sniffed. "Man. I really need to blow my nose."

"Here," Celeste said. She handed him what was left of Andy the Bloated's toilet paper and tried to smile. When Buster was finished, he dropped the tissue into the aisle.

"Thanks," he said.

"You must really love her," Celeste offered.

"I did," Buster said. His voice was hoarse and shaky. "I still do, I guess. I shouldn't have messed around. I don't know. . . . It's hard to let go. You know?"

Celeste wasn't sure what to say. She had never seen a guy cry or confess like this. Not even Edward. It was sort of touching. Especially coming from Buster. She'd written him off as a complete asshole. "Maybe you'll work things out," she said.

"No." Buster sadly shook his head. "Jodi is looking for an Ashley Wilkes, and I'm more like Rhett Butler."

"Well, a lot of girls are looking for Rhett," Celeste said, hoping to cheer him up.

Buster laughed quietly. "Are you?"

Celeste didn't say anything. She didn't really know who she was looking for. Whoever he was, she just hoped he wouldn't have excess gas.

"Hey, you want to watch the rest of the movie with me?" Buster asked. "I mean, we might as well see how it turns out. And I really don't want to be alone."

"Well, gee . . ." She didn't finish. She sort of wanted to see the end of the movie, too. On the other hand, she felt funny sitting here with Buster.

Whatever. The poor guy had been through a lot. And so had she. She awkwardly climbed over him and sat in Jodi's seat, then reached down and picked up the soda cup. "Can I have a sip?" she asked.

"Uh, no—it's flat," Buster said, snatching the cup away from her as she brought it to her lips. "Sorry. It's just not good. Why don't you have some of this instead?"

He reached under his seat and handed her the bottle of rum.

Celeste hesitated. It probably wasn't a good idea to get drunk with Jodi's boyfriend. But who was to say what was a good idea or not anymore? On an existential level, her life had long surpassed the point of absurdity. Her very first college date (or very first heterosexual date, anyway) had farted as she'd kissed him. It was so ridiculous. Celeste had never made a move on anyone before she got to PU . . . and in less than three weeks she'd made two—both of which had ended in disaster. One gay, one gassy. Screw it; she *had* to get drunk. Sartre would have wanted it this way. Or at least Dorothy Parker would have. She took a sip as the lights dimmed. *Mmm.* This stuff was actually pretty good.

"You know, Buster," she said. "I'm sure Jodi really loves you and the two of you will get back together."

Much to her surprise, Buster rested his head on her shoulder. *He must be pretty plastered*, she thought. "I don't think so," he breathed.

Celeste drank a few more sips of rum. Some words were floating on the screen, but Celeste couldn't really read them.

"Hey, you want to get out of here?" Buster asked. "We could go back to my place, you know, just to talk. I could really use some company tonight."

Celeste helped herself to some more rum. Come to think of it, she didn't really want to see the end of the movie as much as she thought she had. And she could use some company tonight as well. She had an *A* to celebrate, and it would be nice just to get her mind off making moves on guys for a little while.

17

Celeste and Buster weren't the only ones drinking rum. Ali and Nice Ed were pretty much up to their eyeballs in it.

"I swear it wasn't what it looked like," Ali said, slumped over the bar at Dimers. She had to shout to make herself heard. A local band, the Athens Greeks, were playing on a small stage in the corner. "It was just one innocent kiss. And I wasn't even the one who initiated it."

Dimers was packed. Tonight there was only one thing cheaper than ten-cent pints of beer, and that was free shots of rum. Captain Morgan[30] was passing them out on a big tray, saying, "Yo ho ho and a bottle of rum," over and over again. But he didn't seem embarrassed at all. He seemed to actually be really into it, like he got off on being Captain Morgan.

"Oh, Pirate Guy," Ali called out over the music.

"Me name is Captain Morgan," he answered in a pirate accent. "Captain Morgan's me name, rum is me game."

□□□□□□□□□□□□□□□□□□□□□□□□□□□□□

30 A promotional double, anyway.

"Rum is me game, too," Ali said. "And I'm winning!" She took two more shots off the pirate's tray for herself and slammed down both of them while Nice Ed and Captain Morgan watched in amazement. Then she ran her fingers through Captain Morgan's wig. "Dude, I love your long, luxurious, curly brown hair," she said.

"Yo ho ho!" Captain Morgan walked away, mumbling something about how much better this job was than his last job playing Santa.

Ali turned back to Nice Ed. "I can't believe I got fired. I didn't even know you could get fired from a volunteer job."

"Well, when Dr. Woo came back and saw you making out with Kid Charlemagne, he was pretty steamed."

"I thought you said he was gone for the night," Ali mumbled. "Anyway, we weren't making out. He's a *chimp,* for Christ's sake. I just kissed him once quickly on the lips because he's so cute. Anybody would've done the same thing."

Ed laughed. "Yeah, but did you have to turn off the lights?"

"Dude, that was a coincidence," Ali said. "I leaned on the light switch by accident."

"Well, you can't blame Woo for thinking what he was thinking," Ed said. "He walks in, the light's off, and you're making out with Kid Charlemagne."

"It was just a peck. You gotta believe me."

"All right, already—I believe you, I believe you," Ed said. He smiled at her and sipped a rum and Coke. "And I'm definitely sorry you won't be back at the animal shelter. We'll miss you a lot, especially me. And especially Kid Charlemagne."

"Well, thank you. It's nice to be missed." She leaned closer to him, nearly toppling off her bar stool. She sort of felt like kissing him. No, no . . . better to wait. She was determined to get a *D* first, so that it would count.

The Athens Greeks finally stopped playing, then made an announcement that their CD, *Toga No Panties,* was available and that their e-mail list was being passed around.

Ali looked at the list when it got to her. People could really be mean.

yousuck@myass.com
pleasestopplaying@myearshurt.com
dieyoufuckers@death.org
www.youaretheworstbandihaveeverheardinmylife.com

There was one semireal e-mail address (satan@pollard.edu) but it was followed by the words: *Please e-mail me and let me know where you are playing so I can know what clubs to avoid. See you in hell, bastards!*

Ali wrote her ex-boss's e-mail address, then passed the list to Ed. She couldn't stop thinking about Kid Charlemagne. Not in *that way,* of course . . . but she was worried that Celeste and Jodi might not let it count, on account of the fact that he wasn't human. But what could she do in the meantime? Suddenly she caught a glimpse of Captain Morgan heading toward the men's room, and it came to her: Captain Morgan started with a *C!* Of course! She lurched from the bar stool and staggered after him. She didn't quite have her sea legs yet. She was weaving from side to side as if she were on a ship in a monsoon.

"Ali?" Nice Ed called. "Ali . . ."

His voice was lost in the din.

When she finally made it to the little hall outside the bathrooms, Captain Morgan helped to steady her.

"Hello, *C*-man," Ali slurred. She batted her eyelashes and smiled.

"Yes, lassie, I'm a man of the sea," Captain Morgan said.

"Whatever." Ali groaned. He was cute, but actually when he started speaking in that captainy way, it was a bit of a turnoff. She opened the men's-room door and dragged him in by his white ruffles. And then she kissed him. She kissed him for a long time, even though his fake handlebar mustache was tickling her nose.

"Wow, lassie," he said.

"Just talk like your regular self," she said.

"Wow, lassie," he said.

Ali decided not to worry about it. Luckily she was drunk enough so that it was an easy decision to make. *I definitely have my* C *now,* she thought. *Hooray!*

Jodi sat backstage in PU's theater department, desperately trying to put her costume together.[31] But industrial green velvet

---

31 The theater was pretty much the only part of her orientation tour she remembered clearly. A girl had hanged herself there. Or something.

was not the easiest thing to work with, especially if you had never sewed anything in your entire life, not even a button. Plus it was really dusty and smelled kind of . . . well, moldy.

"Fuck!" she said out loud to herself. "I mean, oh, fiddle dee dee." She was trying to get into character. She stuck herself with a needle for the tenth time. "Oh, fiddle dee fuck," she said.

Forget it. Maybe she just shouldn't go. Everything about the evening was turning into a complete mess. She had gone to so much trouble, too—first scouring the theater department for an appropriate costume, then finally stealing a stage curtain and practically killing herself in the process. She'd pulled at it with all her strength, and it had come down on top of her, and then she'd cut it and shaped it and sewn it and . . . well, now she supposed she had to wear it.

She stood in front of a full-length mirror and held the "dress" up. Actually it was more like a big moldy green velvet poncho. She slipped it on over her head. Her face fell. *Jesus.* She didn't look like Scarlett, that was for damn sure. And she didn't look like Melanie or Belle Watkins. She didn't even look like Mammy. Unfortunately the only thing she really looked like was the green velvet curtain.

But maybe her future sisters at Kappa Kappa Gamma would see her for the good sport that she was and give her an A for effort—if you considered stealing a curtain and cutting a big hole in it an effort, which Jodi certainly did.

She gathered her curtain up around her ankles and marched off to the ball.

*   *   *

The good news was that nobody noticed how lame Jodi's costume was.

The bad news was that nobody noticed her at all.

She couldn't believe it. Hallie Tosis and lazy-eyed, narcoleptic K. J. Martin were there, but they didn't even so much as say hello. All they did was flash her brittle smiles, then continue chatting with some idiotic sophomore guys. And *they* looked amazing—both were Scarletts, of course, but their dresses were real and very authentic. Jodi sat by herself in the living room and drank screwdrivers until someone announced that it was time for the costume parade. All the freshmen were supposed to line up on the lawn to be judged by the president of the sorority. Whoever won was supposed to walk all around campus making stops at all the other sorority houses. It was sort of like a twisted alcoholic Halloween. Jodi hadn't met the president yet. She was very nervous and excited—and at this point, more than a little drunk. If there was ever a time to prove her worth as a pledge, it was now.

Tonight is the first night of the rest of your life, she reminded herself.

Jodi stumbled out to the lawn and stood in a row with about two dozen perfect Miss Scarletts. Her heart sank. Some of these girls looked as though they had been planning all summer for this party. But whatever. She couldn't let that discourage her. Sure, her costume wasn't exactly the best Miss Scarlett or the most authentic Miss Scarlett—but she certainly did stand out, especially with the fresh new screwdriver stain on the front of her curtain.

All of a sudden she gasped.

The president was making her way toward Jodi. She was slowly walking down the line of Scarletts, looking each one up and down. And Jodi realized something. She knew her. The president of Kappa Kappa Gamma was none other than Augusta DuBitch, from Mandi's party—the same Augusta DuBitch whom Jodi had crowned with vomit and jingle juice.

Jodi swallowed. She was half tempted to bolt, but it was too late to make a run for it now. Maybe Augusta wouldn't remember what had happened. After all, Jodi barely remembered it herself.

Augusta paused in front of her. "Who are you supposed to be?" she asked with a smile.

"I'm the curtain," Jodi said. She felt a flash of hope. Augusta didn't seem angry at all. *Could it be? Could this be my lucky night?*

"I see," Augusta said. "Aren't you also the girl who rubbed puke in my hair?"

Jodi's smile faltered. "I . . . I . . . ."

"Get out of my sight," Augusta snapped.

"But I—"

"Now!"

Jodi ran back into the empty house and burst into tears. She fell on the living-room floor, trying to pull the green poncho off over her head with one hand while reaching for a drink—*any* drink—with the other. She slugged down half of what tasted like whiskey, then managed to free herself from the curtain. She collapsed in a heap on top of it and squeezed her eyes shut.

"Jodi?" a male voice asked.

Her eyes popped open. Zack's hairy head floated in space above her.

"Hey," she said, frowning. "What are *you* doing here?"

Zack shrugged. "I came for the free booze. Here, let me help you up," he offered. He yanked her to her feet. "What's wrong? Why are you crying?"

"I don't think they liked my costume," she said. "And my boyfriend dumped me and then when I agreed to see him, he pissed in a cup and . . . and . . ." Her voice broke.

"Shhh," Zack murmured. "Start from the top. You're not making any sense."

"I need a drink first."

"Good idea," Zack said. "I think the bar's empty, too." He led her to the bar area and grabbed a bottle of tequila and two PU shot glasses.

Jodi downed her shot and immediately poured herself another one, which she swallowed just as fast. The alcohol wasn't affecting her quickly enough. She needed to get blotto.

Zack laughed. "Um, you might want to actually breathe between sips," he said.

"I hate when people tell me to breathe," Jodi grumbled.

"You know, so do I," Zack said. "It's really irritating, like when someone tells you to smile." He poured himself a shot and drank it.

They started matching each other shot for shot. One, two, three.

Soon Jodi was telling him everything. It was like drink-and-dial, only without the phone. She was surprised by how badly she just needed to *talk.* About everything. About her father cutting her off, about her clothes not arriving, about Buster, about Buster's hands, about Mandi's tits, about Augusta's hair . . . *ugh.* When she actually went through it all, it sounded even *worse.* But amazingly enough, Zack listened to everything she said. He was actually almost normal when he wasn't in the dining hall. He was almost *nice.*

"And I just wanted to be in this sorority so much," Jodi concluded. "And now I've blown it. I'll never be in the sister-hood of Kappa Kappa Gamma."

Zack snickered. "Why would you want to pledge a sorority?"

Jodi gaped at him. "Excuse me?"

"You heard me. Why would you want to be a part of *this?*" He waved his shot glass around the bar in disdain. "I mean, you can still get free booze and not be a member. Look at me. I'm not in a sorority—"

"Why wouldn't I want to be a part of it?" Jodi asked, amazed at his stupidity. "There's about a thousand reasons. Living in a beautiful house, making sisters for life, being a part of a great tradition, really belonging somewhere, easy access to free booze—"

"The Greek system is just a mechanism to stifle individuality and freedom," Zack interrupted.

What? English, please. But before she could reply, they were joined by two police officers.

"We're looking for Jodi Stein," one of the cops said.

Jodi laughed. Maybe this was some sort of practical joke. "That's me. Why?" she asked.

"You stole curtains from the theater department. Someone got your license plate number when you drove away. Your car is parked outside this house."

"Silly me," Jodi said, looking at his badge. His name was Officer Davis. He was a *D!* She was up to *D!* What luck!

"Please come with us," the officer said.

Jodi turned to Zack. He smiled reassuringly at her. She shrugged. Good thing she could barely stand. Well, it was a perfect ending to a perfect night. She was on her way to the *slammer*. If she'd once thought Celeste and Ali were bad, what would her prison roommates be like? This was a total nightmare. She *knew* it was a nightmare. Yet for some reason, she couldn't stop smiling. Worse, she couldn't stop staring at Zack's droopy eyelids.

18

The next morning Celeste woke up in a strange bed to find an Indian boy glaring down at her. She screamed. Or she tried to, anyway. All that came out was a pathetic, dry gasp. Her tongue felt like it was made of Velcro. Her head was pounding. She had no idea where she was or what was going on. Her legs were intertwined with another leg and something hard—she looked down—a leg in a cast. And she was naked under the sheet except for socks. Whoever she was with was naked from the waist down except for a Hooters T-shirt—the man she was intertwined with, not the Indian boy—and the man she was intertwined with was . . . oh my God . . .

"Buster!" Celeste exclaimed.

"Shut up." Buster groaned. "My head hurts."

"Get out of here," the Indian boy barked at Celeste. "Buster, what did I tell you about having sex in this room? I can't take it anymore. I'll be forced to report you."

Celeste gasped. She stared at Buster, horrified. Sex? Had she? Had they—

"Get lost, Nanjeeb," Buster muttered.

"Did we have sex?" Celeste whispered.

Buster opened one eye and smiled. "Don't worry, I was gentle. Although you might have a little trouble walking today."

In that instant Celeste came very close to puking all over the bed. But she managed to jump out of bed and scramble into her clothes. Then she ran out of the room. She had no trouble walking. In fact, she had no trouble running as fast as she could. The last thing she heard was Buster yelling after her that she had forgotten to sign his cast.

So was that it? Was she really not a virgin anymore? No. No way. It couldn't count if you couldn't remember a thing about it.

Well, that wasn't totally true. She could remember something. She could remember going back to Buster's room and drinking a mugful of rum and NyQuil[32]—the coughing, sneezing, stuffy head, fever, so you can maybe have sex for the first time with your roommate's ex-boyfriend and not remember it in the morning medicine. . . .

She could remember thinking that Buster could be her *B*.

Oh God, no. No, no, no. Please, no.

Before she knew it, she'd reached Maize. She dashed upstairs to the triple and headed straight for the bathroom. She looked at herself in the mirror, panting. Did she look different? More womanly? Not really. No. She just looked pale

32 Cherry flavored (yummy).

and tired and puffy. So there was a very good chance that she *hadn't* had sex. Right. Although she was starting to get a little bit of eczema on her left cheek from stress. . . .

This was a fiasco. The worst day of her life. She hadn't been in love, she hadn't done any of the things she had read about in the *Kama Sutra* and planned to do. Hell, she couldn't even *remember* it. If it had even happened. So did it count or did it not count? In a way, she wanted it to count so she could no longer be a virgin, but on the other hand, she definitely wanted a do-over. So it *didn't* count.

She stumbled out of the bathroom and slumped down on her bed. The very first thing she saw was the picture of Jodi and Buster in its silver frame. *Shit.* How could she face Jodi now?

And where *was* Jodi?

Jodi's bed looked as though it hadn't been slept in. Actually, so did Ali's. The room was exactly the way Celeste had left it the day before.

Shower! That's what she needed more than anything, a shower. She could take a hot shower and think about what to do.

Or maybe she could just lie down and go to sleep. . . .

When Celeste came to again, Ali and Jodi were sitting on their beds, staring at her.

"Hey, where were you guys?" Celeste asked groggily. She sat up straight and yawned. "I was worried about you." She really *had* been worried—mostly that Jodi had found Buster, and Buster had told her what had happened.

Ali smiled. "It looks like we all had quite a night last night, y'all," she said. "We all look terrible. Hey, Jodi, what's that black stuff on your fingers?"

"I was arrested and fingerprinted," Jodi said. "I spent the night in jail."

"What?" Ali and Celeste shouted at the same time.

And then the whole story came tumbling out of Jodi's mouth. Buster had peed in the soda cup in the movie theater, breaking her heart for the second time in two weeks, and then, in true Scarlett O'Hara fashion, she had stolen the curtains from the movie theater, gotten bombed at the party, been yelled at by Augusta DuBitch, been arrested and fingerprinted, and was about to be released, when she'd done an unbelievably stupid thing. She'd tried to kiss the police officer who had arrested her, Officer Davis, because he was a *D* and she was up to *D,* but instead of kissing her back, he had gotten angry and accused her of trying to bribe a police officer and had thrown her in a jail cell with a hooker named Brandy who made Hallie Tosis's breath smell like a mountain of York peppermint patties in comparison.

Jodi took a deep breath. "And now I'm here," she said.

Celeste's jaw hung open.

"Dude," Ali said.

"So what's going to happen?" Celeste asked. "I mean, is there going to be a trial—"

"No, no. Don't worry. The school agreed to drop the charges if I promised to pay for new velvet curtains to the tune of two thousand dollars."

"TWO THOUSAND DOLLARS?" Ali shouted. "DUDE!"

"How are you going to do that?" Celeste asked.

"Well, I just couldn't call my father, so I stopped at this hair salon and I asked how much I could get for selling my hair. Do you know what they said?"

"What?" Celeste asked, getting really upset now. She couldn't stand the idea of Jodi selling her hair like Jo in *Little Women*.

"That all I'd get was thirty-five bucks."

Ali shook her head, aghast. "Thirty-five bucks? That's it? What'd you say?"

"I said thirty-five bucks, fuck you," Jodi said. "And then I sold my car."

Celeste and Ali looked at each other. They were absolutely speechless.

"Come on, girls, it's not like someone *died*," Jodi mumbled.

None of them said anything for what seemed like a really long time.

Celeste was suddenly overcome with guilt. *Poor Jodi.* How could Celeste possibly have had sex with Buster like that behind Jodi's back? Jodi must never find out. Never, ever. Not in a million years. Celeste swore that she would never tell. Even if it meant being on *A* for the rest of her life. If she didn't remember being with Buster, it didn't count. Period. Maybe they should add that to the list of rules. . . .

"How did you get home?" Ali finally asked Jodi.

"Zack drove me," Jodi said. "He was really great. I mean,

he's a geek, but I don't think I would have survived without him."

"Hey, who's *Zack?*" Ali asked.

Before Jodi could answer, the phone rang.

"Don't answer it," Celeste warned. "I think it could be that guy Fredo from the kitchen again. There were four messages from him when I got home."

The machine picked up. *Beep!*

"Hi, Celeste, it's Buster. Listen, thanks for last night. You were great, really. I just wanted to let you know I found your bra. I'll hang it on the doorknob outside my door so you can get it anytime. Anyway, thanks again. Oh, and hi, Jodi."

Celeste's heart began to pound. Her face turned bright red.

"What the hell is that all about?" Jodi shrieked.

"Jo-Jodi, I'm so sorry," Celeste stammered. She felt like she was a character in some Shakespearean tragedy. Either that or a bad episode of *Undeclared.* "I should have told you."

"You're *sorry?*" Jodi screamed. "You're sorry you slept with my boyfriend?"

"Ex-boyfriend," Celeste said automatically. "But I'm not even really sure I slept with him. I'm almost positive I didn't, actually."

Jodi's eyes blazed. "What? Not sure? How is that *possible?*"

"I was drunk."

"So? Jesus! Even *kissing* him would be bad enough! I thought I was going to *marry* him! How could you *do* that?"

"I'm sorry," Celeste repeated. "Really. I didn't know what I was doing—"

"You know, that's some act you pull," Jodi hissed.

Celeste blinked. "Act? What do you mean?"

"The innocent girl from the Upper West Side. *That* act! It's all horseshit! You're a schemer and a slut and . . . and . . ."

"Jodi, you're not being fair," Celeste said, finding herself becoming defensive. "Please."

"Fair!" Jodi yelled. How could Celeste even *talk* about fair? She wasn't just mad, she wasn't just irate, she wasn't just horrified . . . she didn't know *what* she was.

Celeste hung her head. "If you hadn't abandoned Buster at the movie theater to steal those curtains, none of this would have happened," she muttered.

Jodi stared at her. "Is that the best excuse you can come up with?" she demanded.

"Y'all, come on," Ali interjected. The last thing she wanted was to be caught in the middle of some dumb fight over an ape. Until now the triple had been her only real sanctuary. The one place she could truly relax. "We can all work this out."

"I don't think so," Jodi snapped.

"Come on, let me tell you about my night," Ali offered.

"There is no excuse for what you did," Jodi said to Celeste. Her voice trembled. She strode toward the door. "And you can both forget about that stupid hookup game because it's *over*."

"But it can't be over!" Ali cried, desperately trying to

ease the tension. "Check it out, y'all. I'm already up to *E*. I got *C, D,* and *E* in one night. Captain Morgan, Don—the drummer of this band called the Athens Greeks—and this nice guy Ed I told you about, who's the vet-in-training at the animal shelter."

But Jodi was too infuriated to care. She stormed out of the room.

Jodi spent the night next door, drinking sex-on-the-beaches and smoking a fat joint with lazy-eyed, narcoleptic K. J. Martin and Hallie Tosis. *Fuck Celeste,* she thought. *Fuck everybody. From now on I'm looking out for number one.* Unfortunately, right before she passed out on their sheepskin rug, she managed to break Hallie's karaoke machine, singing "I Will Survive" at the top of her lungs. It might be mid-September, but it felt like July Fourth. Independence Day. She was done with Buster and two-faced Celeste and sticking-up-for-two-faced Celeste's friend Ali. She was free of them all.

Meanwhile, next door, yet a million miles away, Ali and Celeste barely said anything to each other. They were too depressed.

The next morning Ali and Celeste were rudely awakened by two freaky blond girls who burst into their room wearing rain-coats.

"What the fuck?" Ali said—and the next thing she knew, they were being hosed down with a fire extinguisher. White foam covered everything in the whole room.

"K. J. Martin and Hallie Thompson!" one of the blondes shouted. "This is your call to rush Kappa Kappa Gamma!"

"Excuse me," Ali said. "We are not K. J. Martin or Hallie Tosis. Do we look disgusting?"

"Do we have lazy eyes?" Celeste asked.

"Do we have bad breath?" Ali added.

The girls looked at each other.

"Must have gotten the wrong room," the first one said.

"Sorry," the other girl said.

They slammed the door behind them.

Ali and Celeste surveyed the damage. They looked at Jodi's empty bed. It was covered in foam. That could be cleaned up, though.

Getting Jodi back—that would be a little harder.

19

For the next few weeks, all the way up to midterms, Jodi went out of her way to avoid Celeste. She only used the triple for sleeping. Period. In fact, she found herself spending more and more time with lazy-eyed, narcoleptic K. J. Martin and Hallie Tosis. In spite of their obvious flaws, they were actually pretty nice. Well, maybe that was pushing it. Hallie was the more annoying of the two. Definitely. She was always saying things like, "Golly, my *SHED*-ule is really *chockers*"—as if Jodi was supposed to know what that meant. But they did have one very important thing in common: they were all pledging Kappa Kappa Gamma.

Still, hanging out with them wasn't the same as hanging out with her roomies. Jodi missed them—well, not Celeste. But she missed being part of their little group. It was strange how attached she had become to them in such a short time and how much she had enjoyed their secret society . . . especially considering how much she'd hated them that first crazy day, when Celeste's parents were doling out pot and waving around a sage stick. It seemed like such a long time ago. She felt like a completely different person now. She had really been through a lot since then. She'd lost Buster. She'd gotten her first job. She'd been arrested. She'd sold her car. Celeste and Ali had been there to share all of it. So actually, they had been through a lot *together*. They were her true friends—well, except for Celeste.

And now, sitting in the library and lamely attempting to study, Jodi once again found herself thinking about them. This was not part of the plan. No, the plan was to work: to roll up her sleeves—well, roll up Hallie's sleeves, anyway—and pull an all-nighter. (Hallie had been nice enough to lend Jodi clothes, as Jodi's stuff now pretty much seemed lost forever. She'd even stopped bothering to call the mail room and UPS. What was the point? So somebody could call her "ma'am" again and put her on hold?)

Jodi pulled out her Filofax to look at her things-to-do section. She accidentally opened to the Alphabetical Hookup List.

"What's that?"

Jodi flinched. She turned around to see Zack standing behind her. Her face instantly turned red. Why did he always seem to appear out of nowhere? He must be stalking her. Okay, maybe not *stalking*. . . .

"Nothing," Jodi mumbled, quickly closing the book.

Zack smirked. "Nothing?" He pulled out the chair beside her and sat down. He smelled of cigarillos. The scent actually wasn't so bad when it was on someone's clothes. "So, what are you doing in the library? I've never seen you here before."

Jodi shrugged. "Trying to study," she said.

"Can't study in your room, huh?" Zack nodded to himself. "I had the same problem freshman year. It's impossible to get anything done with roommates around."

"Yeah," Jodi said in a faraway voice. "Impossible."

Zack's brow furrowed. "Is something wrong?"

"Have you ever had a best friend who did something really bad to you and then became your ex-friend?" Jodi heard herself ask. She couldn't believe it. The question had just popped out of her mouth, as if somebody else were doing the talking. She suddenly felt silly, like Cindy Brady asking Greg Brady's advice.

"Did old Stonewall Jackson do something mean to you?" Zack asked, smiling.

Maybe it was the diet pills she had taken to help her study, or maybe it was Zack's eyes and the way he was smiling at her like that, or maybe it was the fact that his hair was about four inches tall—but whatever it was, Jodi started spilling her guts to him again. She told Zack everything about what had happened between her and Celeste.[33] She told him all about how she had really found herself *liking* Celeste, too—the way they'd hung out, sharing alphabet soup, listening to their next-door neighbors hook up with stupid guys . . . but now those days were over. For good.

33 Except for the part about creating the Alphabetical Hookup List, of course.

"So what do you think?" Jodi concluded.

Zack leaned back in his chair and stroked his chin. "Well, if you really want to know, I think you might be overreacting," he said.

"What?" Jodi shrieked.

"Shhh," Zack whispered, giggling. "This is a library, remember?"

Jodi frowned. "Well, explain what you mean."

"It *is* pretty sleazy to sleep with your friend's ex so soon after a breakup," Zack conceded. "But this is college. Once you cut a guy loose, he's fair game. I mean, this school is built on hormones. You know that. Your next-door neighbors are prime examples. Besides, maybe Celeste was really upset about something. Maybe she really *was* so drunk that she couldn't remember. I bet she feels terrible."

"Yeah, but . . ." Jodi didn't finish. It was true that she hadn't really given Celeste time to explain herself. If Celeste *had* been really upset about something, then maybe she *would* have gotten so drunk that she'd black out. Besides, Jodi hadn't exactly been discouraging Celeste from fooling around with guys. She and Ali had been pretty much egging Celeste on to get laid as soon as possible. In a subtle, supportive way, but still. . . .

"Are you still interested in Buster?" Zack asked, looking her right in the eye.

Jodi was a little taken aback by the question. It was pretty personal. But she thought about it for a minute. Mostly she thought about watching Buster drunkenly fill up a cup with his pee. "No, I'm not," she said. And she meant it.

"Well, good. Because it sounds like this Buster is a real zero. Right?"

"Right," Jodi said, suddenly realizing he *was* right. Buster *was* a real zero. The genuine article. In fact, she could kiss Buster again when she got to the end of her list so that he could be her *Z* for *Zero*. Unless her *Z* was Zack—

Wait a second. What am I thinking?

"So maybe you should think about forgiving Celeste," Zack said.

Jodi blinked at him. Deep in her heart, she knew that Zack was right. Buster was an asshole, and they'd all be better off without him. And maybe she *had* overreacted. But she wasn't sure if she could forgive Celeste. Not without some kind of gesture on Celeste's part. A *big* gesture. Like a new car. Okay, maybe not that big. But something.

Who had ever heard of a surprise field trip?

More important, who had ever heard of a surprise field trip to a morgue?

Ali stood with her biology class outside a big metal door in the fluorescent bowels of Athens General Hospital while their teacher, Professor Rinaldi, tried to get their attention. He sort of looked like a corpse himself—skeletal and hideously pale, with glasses that were like the eye sockets of a skull. Or at least, that was how they seemed to Ali.

"Okay, class, now for your special surprise," Professor

Rinaldi said. "If we're lucky, we'll be able to watch an autopsy performed on a real corpse!" He actually sounded all jazzed up about it, like they were all going to get a big bang out of the experience.

A couple of kids ran back upstairs.

"I don't know about this," Ali whispered to Cute Jason.

Cute Jason (so named because he had big blue eyes and the most adorable brown curls and also used the word *dude*—always a plus) smiled at her. "Oh, we should definitely do it. It'll be good experience for you if you're thinking of becoming a vet."

Ali smiled back. "You're right," she said.

She followed her class through the big metal door. The morgue was smaller than she'd thought it would be, but there were still those same big refrigerated body drawers you always saw in the movies. It was pretty damn morbid. Especially with Professor Rinaldi beaming from ear to ear like a kid in a candy store. Maybe this wasn't the worst thing in the world, but it wasn't exactly Christmas.

Professor Rinaldi led them into a small operating room.

Ali braced herself. There was a dead guy on the table. Well, she was pretty sure it was a dead guy. He was covered with a white sheet, which Professor Rinaldi took upon himself to remove.

Holy—

FI: The dude was dead. Ali tried not to gag. It was a man. Just a regular white guy, but he was dead. His eyes were closed and his mouth was turned down in a slight frown. He had sort of a kind face. Ali suddenly felt bad for him that he was lying there frowning. She wanted to turn up the corners of his mouth into a smile.

A girl standing by his feet said, "Look, he has a tag on his toe, just like in the movies."

"That's his ID tag," Professor Rinaldi said.

"Duh," someone added.

"What's his name?" someone else asked.

Ali started to really feel bad for the guy. He didn't need to be lying there dead while a bunch of obnoxious college kids made fun of him.

"His name is Fred," the girl said. "Fred Doe."

Cute Jason chuckled.

An older man dressed in a lab coat entered the room. "We just call him Fred Doe because he was a DOA and he didn't have any ID on him. We already had a John Doe, so the EMS worker gave him the name Fred."

"He doesn't look like a Fred," a kid said. "That's such a dorky name."

"I think he looks like a Trevor," the girl said. "Or a Steve or a Parker. You know, like something soap opera."

Ali's head started spinning. She wondered if she was going to puke. She felt terrible for this Fred. He had family somewhere who didn't even know he was dead. This was a real person lying here. It wasn't a joke.

"Sorry, Fred," she whispered.

Wait a second. Fred began with an *F.*

Suddenly she felt sick. *Really* sick. Good Lord, what was

she thinking? What was happening to her? She didn't know. She didn't *want* to know. So she bolted. Everything around her just went blank—and she ran out of the room, through the morgue, up the stairs, out of the hospital, and out onto the street. *What would Jodi and Celeste say if they knew that I actually thought about getting my* F *by kissing a corpse?* That would make for some interesting conversation over shots of tequila. And she did love to shock them. They were both such naive girls in their own ways. . . .

But then she remembered. They weren't even really doing the Alphabetical Hookup List anymore. Jodi and Celeste weren't on speaking terms with each other, and they were barely even talking to her. How had everything gotten so awful, just when things had been going so well? They had all been getting along great, and then Celeste had slept with Buster, and now it was all a big mess.

And there was nothing Ali could do about it.[34]

She had tried talking to both of them together. Then separately. Then not talking at all. Then leaving notes. Everything she tried ended up failing. She couldn't patch up the triple. It was making her crazy. She had almost just kissed a dead man, for Christ's sake. She was really losing it. And she knew precisely why, too. For a brief moment in time—for those first few fun nights they'd shared in the triple—Ali had felt something she had never felt before: at home.

Now it was all disappearing.

□□□□□□□□□□□□□□□□□□□□□□□□□□□□□□□□

34 A therapist once told her that children of divorce tend to want to be "problem solvers."

"Ali! Dude!"

Cute Jason was running down the sidewalk, calling to her.

Ali hung her head in shame.

"What happened in there?" Cute Jason panted, gasping for breath.

"I'm sorry," Ali said. "I just . . . I just got a little freaked out. That's all."

"Don't be sorry. Dude, who would take their class to a morgue? You did what everybody else wanted to do. You were shaken. That's perfectly understandable."

Ali laughed. "You're not going to start singing 'Wind Beneath My Wings,' are you?"

"Dude, I mean it," Cute Jason said. "I can tell that you're a sensitive type. You should come work with me at the Wrinkled Peach sometime."

She couldn't tell if he was being serious or not. "What's that? A bar or something?"

"No, it's a retirement home. It's really called the Ringfield Peach, but everyone who works there calls it the Wrinkled Peach."

Interesting, Ali thought. She certainly had plenty of time on her hands now that she wasn't allowed to work at the animal shelter. And even if the Alphabetical Hookup List was on hold for a while for Celeste and Jodi, there was no reason for *her* not to continue with it. The retirement home would be a great place to make up the ground she'd lost kissing all those lesbians. After all, old guys just *loved* college girls. And maybe if Jodi and Celeste learned that Ali was still playing, they'd join in again and everything would go back to normal.

"Hey, you wanna get some lunch or something?" Cute Jason asked. "I don't really feel like going back down to the morgue, you know?"

"Sure," Ali said. "Running makes me work up a real appetite."

"Me too," Cute Jason said flirtatiously.

"Me three," Ali said, flirting right back.

20

The coast was clear. Celeste and Ali were out somewhere, so Jodi could spend a few minutes in the triple. She was surprised at how much she really missed the old place. But now was not the time to dredge up all of that. Now she had to get ready and get going.

First she put on lipstick—Bombshell, by M•A•C—then fluffed up her hair a little. Her outfit was kind of understated: just jeans and a sweater, another Hallie-slash-K. J. combo, but it didn't matter. She was just meeting Zack, after all. It wasn't a date or anything. She was letting him "make up" for the Stonewall Jackson watermelon incident. She was supposed to meet him at some place called the 'Vous. He had called her earlier that evening with a cryptic invitation to do something "mind expanding."

Jodi didn't want to give Zack the wrong idea. This *wasn't* a date. But she *was* curious about the whole mind-expanding scenario, so she had said she would go. She definitely wasn't interested in going out to places with him on a regular basis, though. For one thing, it was way too soon to behave normally after being dumped by Buster, and for another thing—the more important thing—Zack was . . . well, weird.

Anyway, it was all academic. There was another Kappa Kappa Gamma pledge party tonight, starting at midnight, so the mind-expanding experience would have its own Cinderella-style time limit. Right. At midnight she was out of there, no matter how expanded her mind was. There was no way she was going to miss this party or blow it in any way after the Scarlett O'Hara fiasco. Which was another reason why it was kind of good that her outfit was understated. She didn't exactly need to be drawing a lot of attention to herself.

She would just go to the party and blend in. Just one of the sisters. A perfect fit.

There was a knock on the door.

Jodi hesitated. For a second she worried that it might be Celeste, but then she remembered that Celeste lived here, so she wouldn't knock. Not to mention the fact that people who had sex with other people's boyfriends usually weren't the kind of people who knocked anyway. Besides, it was Saturday night, so Celeste and Ali were probably out.

She was right: it wasn't her roommates. It was lazy-eyed, narcoleptic K. J. Martin.

"Can I borrow your hot plate? Hallie and I are going to make hot buttered rum for the big Kappa Kappa Gamma pledge party tonight."

"They asked you to bring it?" Jodi said, puzzled.

"Yeah, well, *told* us," lazy-eyed, narcoleptic K. J. said. "Someone delivered a message from Augusta telling us to bring it. We're really excited. It's an honor to be told to do something for our future sisters." Her sleepy eyes glazed over. "Hallie's over at the house now, cleaning the bathrooms for the party. It's a rare honor."

That's strange, Jodi thought. Nobody had given her any messages to do anything. Maybe Augusta was still mad. Jodi would be thrilled to clean Augusta's bathroom if she wanted her to—anything to make it up to her for accidentally rubbing puke in her hair.

Jodi handed over the hot plate.

"You know what, maybe I'll make it in here, if you don't mind. Our room kind of smells like ass," lazy-eyed, narcoleptic K. J. Martin said.

"Whatever," Jodi said, distracted. "I'll see you at midnight."

"See you at midnight," lazy-eyed, narcoleptic K. J. Martin echoed—as if she were Jodi's lazy-eyed, narcoleptic fairy godmother.

Once again, as usual, Celeste found herself combing the campus alone at night, avoiding Buster and looking for Jodi. Now she was passing Hackman and heading toward the big dining hall. She had to apologize to Jodi once and for all. She couldn't go on like this. She had been wrong to sleep with Buster, even if it hadn't been entirely her fault. She shouldn't have even flirted with him. No way was she going to ruin a potentially great friendship with Jodi and Ali over a jerk like Buster. She had to try to find a way to make Jodi understand and forgive her. And she definitely—DEFINITELY— knew that she would never, ever touch a single drop of rum as long as she lived.

Sirens sounded in the distance, adding to Celeste's loneliness. It reminded her of being home in New York. The lonely sound of a siren going by, reminding you of all the terrible things going on in the world and how you were powerless to stop them.

Maybe she would go by the triple one more time.

Celeste walked up the hill toward Maize. She stopped dead in her tracks when she saw the dorm. Something was very wrong. Maize was surrounded by fire trucks and firemen. There were ladders and hoses and whirring red lights. Smoke was pouring from a window on the second floor. What the hell was going on? She saw Hallie Tosis talking to a fireman, and she ran up to them, hoping to get some information.

"Oh, hi, Celeste, this is Casey O'Rourke—he's a firefighter," Hallie Tosis said.

Actually, Celeste had figured that out for herself, due to the fact that he was wearing a full fireman's uniform, complete with big boots, a black coat with a yellow stripe, and a fireman's hat—not to mention that he was holding a big yellow ax.

"He's a modern-time hero," Hallie continued. Luckily the smell of smoke masked the stench of her breath. "How can we thank you, Mr. Nine-one-one? Fireman Casey, you're a super*stah!*"

"Uh, I've really got work to do here," the fireman said.

"What happened?" Celeste asked.

"A fire in room 213," the fireman said.

Celeste's heart squeezed. She must have heard him incorrectly. "Excuse me?"

"A fire in room 213," he repeated.

"That's my room!" she shrieked. She was so upset, she didn't even think about the fact that the fireman's name was Casey and that he was handsome and that she was up to *C*.

At that moment Celeste caught a glimpse of a very frazzled lazy-eyed, narcoleptic K. J. Martin. She was hobbling out of the dorm, wrapped in a black blanket.

"Are you okay?" Celeste asked.

Lazy-eyed, narcoleptic K. J. Martin nodded, looking sheepish. For some reason, she wouldn't look Celeste in the eye. "Look, I'm sorry," she said. "I was . . . well, um, see, I was cooking something on Jodi's bed. See, I borrowed her hot plate. And, uh—well, I don't know if you know this, but I have narcolepsy. It's not my fault. It's a medical condition that I can't control. I mean, I guess I should have had better sense. . . ." Her voice trailed off.

Celeste was flabbergasted. "Was anybody hurt?" she asked.

Lazy-eyed, narcoleptic K. J. Martin shook her head. "No. I was alone. I woke up and ran out of there, but Jodi's bed is toast."

"It's as crisp as a crumpet," Hallie Tosis added.

"It's as fried as a Mexican banana," lazy-eyed, narcoleptic K. J. Martin said, staring at her feet.

Oh my God, Celeste thought.

"Don't worry," Fireman Casey said. "Only one bed was damaged. Everything else survived."

A wave of relief washed over Celeste. "So you're sure that nobody was hurt?"

Fireman Casey grinned. "Well, *that* guy got a little over-heated. . . ." He pointed to the bronze statue of the Buddha, standing in the grass near the fire truck. Another fireman was hosing it off with water. His head was melted down to nothing, but his stomach was still there. Celeste sighed. The Alphabetical Hookup rules were safe. Jodi and Ali were safe.

But where on earth were they, anyway?

As it turned out, the Wrinkled Peach was a creepy place and not exactly Ali's idea of a fun Saturday night. Cleaning bedpans did have a sort of Zen thing going for it when you got into the rhythm of it—dump, rinse, rinse again, stack, dump, rinse, rinse again, stack—but it had inherent limitations, and it smelled stinky. Question: Why did all her volunteer jobs have to involve picking up shit? Celeste's dad would probably know the answer. It was probably some karmic thing for being a villain in a past life or something.

It was fun being with Cute Jason, though.

"Why don't I finish this up and you go out there and mingle," he said. "Meet the people. Spread some joy."

"You sure?" she asked.

He nodded, his cute blue eyes as cute as ever.

"Um . . . okay."

Ali left the room and walked tentatively down the hall. She wasn't sure what crazies she would come across. The place definitely had a strange vibe to it; if it hadn't been featured on *20/20* or *60 Minutes* yet, it probably would be soon. At the end of the hall was a living room with a TV going and three men playing cards. They looked pretty normal, except for the fact that they were all wearing matching striped pajamas and slippers, sort of like white-haired triplets. Maybe they *were* triplets. She paused at the door, then wandered inside.

"Hi," she said.

The three men barely looked up.

"I'm Alison Sheppard, a new volunteer here," she offered, feeling extremely dorky.

"You got any money?" one of them asked. He spoke very softly, with a rasp.

"Sorry," Ali said.

"We can play for sexual favors," another one said. He was tall and skinny.

Ali laughed uncomfortably. It certainly would be a *favor*. "I don't know," she said.

"Well, would you mind moving? You're blocking the boob tube," the third man said.

Ali stepped aside so she wouldn't be standing in front of the TV. She noticed that an episode of *Sex and the City* was on.

"You like that show?" the third man asked.

"Yeah," Ali said. Truth be told, she'd only watched five minutes of it once, and it had kind of annoyed her. "I mean, I don't know. I guess."

"I love it. My granddaughter sends me the shows on tape so I never have to miss one. This place is too cheap to have Home Box Office. You want to see a picture of her?"

"Okay," Ali said. She thought it was cute the way he said Home Box Office instead of HBO. And she thought it was cute that he was going to show her a picture of his granddaughter. She had a feeling that if she worked here, she'd see a lot of pictures of grandchildren.

"Here it is," the man said, struggling to pull his wallet out of the pocket of his bathrobe. He held the wallet open so Ali could see the picture. But it wasn't a picture of his granddaughter in the clear plastic sleeve. It was a picture of Sarah Jessica Parker. "She's my favorite," he said. "I'll show her Mr. Big if she wants to see him. He's right here in my pajamas."

"I like the big blonde," another one said.

"I like that redhead lawyer. She's a little dykey, but I like that nice flat chest."

"We should introduce ourselves," old man number one said. "I'm Harry. And this is George and Frank. We welcome you to the Wrinkled Peach."

"Harry, George, and Frank," Ali said. Then she smiled. *F, G,* and *H.* The next three letters that she needed. This was such an evil game! Men were starting to mean nothing more than a letter to her. Of course, these men were horny old goats, so that made her feel a little better. They were sort of fascinating, in a way. She'd always assumed that once men got older, they lost their interest in sex. Apparently not.

"You play gin?" Harry asked.

Ali pulled up a chair and sat down at the table. "Deal me in," she said.

"We can't play for nothing," Frank said. "How about we play strip?"

"Strip gin?" Ali asked. She tried not to grimace. She was wearing a few layers, but she doubted these guys were wearing underwear under their pajamas. On the other hand, playing strip gin was better than cleaning bedpans. "Well . . . okay."

Cute Jason walked into the room. He was holding a video camera. "Well, well, dudes," he said, winking at Ali. "What have we here?"

Ali smiled. "I'm mingling and spreading joy, just like you said to do," she said.

"She sure is," Frank said.

"Well, sorry to interrupt," Cute Jason said with a smirk. "Ali, come with me."

The three old men groaned. Ali shrugged and stood up. But before she left, she had something to take care of. She bent over and kissed each man on the lips, then ran out into the hall. Cute Jason grabbed her arm and pulled her into an empty patient's room.

"What was that all about?" he cried.

"Spreading joy," Ali said. "Just like you said."

He burst out laughing. "You're crazy," Cute Jason said.

"Well, you should be happy because I'm up to *J*." (Her *I* was taken care of from sleeping with Ian Haas.)

"What does that mean?" Cute Jason asked.

"Nothing," Ali said, smiling. "What's the video camera for?" she asked.

"I'm trying to make a documentary about the people here," he said. "But you know what my film is missing?"

"What?" Ali asked.

"A sex scene."

Ali arched an eyebrow. "That's terrible," she murmured. She closed the door, then reached over and flicked out the light. The room went pitch black. "Every good documentary about an old folks' home should have a sex scene."

21

"I don't know, Zack," Jodi said, practically yelling to make herself heard over the pulsating thump of techno. She surveyed the crowd of dancing kids. They all looked like clones of Ali—except that most of them were wearing large crucifixes. "This place is kind of lame."

"Well, that's why I brought this," Zack said. He held out his palm.

Jodi looked down at the little white aspirin-size pill resting there. It looked like the pearl she'd found once in an oyster when she was a kid on the beach in East Quogue. That had been one of the most exciting days of her life.

"You want me to do Ecstasy?" she asked.

"Only if you want to," Zack said. "I wanted to bring you to this Christian rave because I thought it would be fun for us. Nobody else here is on drugs. But you know, since neither one of us is Christian—I'm an atheist and you're a bat mitzvah—I thought that might give us license to try Ecstasy. Well, I've done it once before."

A strobe light started flickering. Jodi's head was already spinning, even without the drug. She was a little nervous, but she knew she wouldn't get through four years of college without trying Ecstasy. She might as well jump in and get it over with. And they had to do *something* to make this Christian thing fun.

"Will it wear off by midnight?" she asked.

"Probably a little after," Zack said. "I'm really not sure."

"Why not?" Jodi said. The Kappa Kappa Gamma pledge party would probably be more fun on X as well. She took the tiny pill from Zack's hand and washed it down with a small bottle of water. The bottle had cost her three dollars. The words *I Love Jesus* were printed on it.

They'd danced together for about fifteen minutes, when suddenly Jodi felt a wave of something strange and hot and overpowering, like a blanket. Her heart began to pound. She had a hard time catching her breath. She also realized she was grinding her teeth.

"Are you okay?" Zack asked.

"I don't know," Jodi said. Little flashes of light scuttled at the edges of her vision. "Um, I think I just need a breath of fresh air."

"Here, follow me," Zack said. He took her hand and led her to the bathroom. She could feel his fingers pulsating in time to the music.

Boys and girls were staring at her. Their faces blended together grotesquely, shimmering with a purple glow. There was definitely something wrong with the concept of the coed bathroom. Sometimes a girl just needed to be alone. Especially when she was hallucinating and couldn't breathe. . . .

"Oh God. Oh God," she whispered.

"Just give it a minute," Zack said. "I feel it, too. E can come on strong. There's nothing to worry about, though. In a few seconds you'll get used to it and feel better, and then it'll be amazing."

Jodi nodded. Surprisingly, his words soothed her. She started to breathe evenly. But she had a long ways to go to "amazing."

Then all at once things started to lighten up. Literally. She felt light, like she was floating. Like that scene in the movie *Willie Wonka and the Chocolate Factory* where Charlie and his grandfather are floating in this room and the only way to come down to the ground is to wish it or say something silly. She found herself floating back onto the dance floor. Zack followed. A song from the movie—the one that those Oompa Loompas sang—began to ring over and over in her head in perfect unison to the beat.

Oompa Loompa doodley doo,
I've got some Ec-sta-sy for you.
Oompa Loompa doodly dee,
If you are wise, you will do it with me.

"What?" Zack asked, laughing.

Jodi's eyes widened. "Did I sing that out loud?"

"Uh, yeah," Zack said. "Have you ever considered becoming a poet?"

She laughed, too. "You're right. I feel a lot better now."

They danced and danced and danced. Zack's hair was like a wildfire burning in the night. Jodi took his hands and twirled beneath his upraised arms.

"Jodi?"

"Yes, Zacky?"

"Are you having fun?"

"Hey, look!" She dragged Zack off the dance floor and over to a doorway where a string of round, yellow smiley face lights were hung. The smiley faces looked strange for some reason; they had small strips of black masking tape covering their eyes like little blindfolds. "That's so weird," Jodi said. She stared at them for a really long time, deeply contemplating their weirdness.

A boy walked by, holding a Bible.

"Look," Jodi said to the boy.

They all stood and contemplated the yellow smiley face lights together.

"Happy faces see no evil," the boy said, extremely slowly.

"What?" Jodi said.

"Happy faces see no evil," the boy said again.

"They don't?" Jodi asked, genuinely fascinated. "Why not?"

"Because they're optimistic," the boy said.

"Ooh. That's so interesting." Jodi turned to Zack. "Zacky?"

"Jodi, don't call me Zacky," Zack said.

"Okay. Happy faces see no evil because they're optimistic," Jodi said, like a parrot on Ecstasy. "Isn't that interesting?"

Zack laughed. "Yeah, it kinda is," he said.

Jodi put her arms around his neck and started slowly dancing with him, even though the beat of the music was fast and furious. She had her own beat in her head. Her own drummer. Her own philosopher. Her own Zack. She had never noticed how yellow those smiley faces were. Or how tall and strong Zack was. Or how deep and brown his eyes were. They were like the chocolates in the chocolate factory.

Jodi put her face very close to his and brushed his cheek with her eyelash.

"What was that?" Zack asked.

"Butterfly fuck," Jodi said. "That's how butterflies fuck." She emphasized the word *fuck* very sexily.

Zack pulled away from her slightly. "Um . . . okay," he said.

"Let's be butterflies," Jodi said. "I feel so good." Aside from feeling good, Jodi was also feeling incredibly attracted to Zack. *Sexually* attracted to him. In fact, she had never wanted anyone so much in her entire life. With her arms still wrapped around his neck, Jodi stood up on tiptoe and kissed Zack on the lips. It was a hot, soft, sweet kiss.

"Jodi, don't," he whispered. "That's the pill talking. Let's not ruin this. We're friends."

"What?" Jodi said, confused. She stopped dancing. She didn't get it. "Of course we're friends. But why does that mean—"

"Jodi, this isn't the time to talk about it."

"What? Why not?"

Zack just looked down at the floor. He refused to continue the conversation. He wouldn't answer her. What was wrong with him? What was wrong with *her*? That was the real question. *Screw this,* she thought. She looked at her watch. *Oh my God!* It was already eleven forty-five. And she was still tripping! Or rolling, or wasted, or whatever they called it. She had to get out of here. She had to go to Kappa Kappa Gamma. Immediately.

She turned and bolted from the club.

"Jodi!" Zack called after her. "Wait!"

But she was already bursting through the doors and out into the street. She shivered once in the night air. The streetlights sparkled with a curious brightness. She hesitated, looking in both directions, then laughed out loud. She had no idea which way she should go to Kappa Kappa Gamma. So why was she laughing? It wasn't funny. . . .

A group of girls strolled past her on the sidewalk. Jodi's dilated eyes bulged. Jesus must definitely be on her side tonight! One of the girls was Augusta DuBois. She ran to catch up with them. This was so perfect.

"Hey!" she cried breathlessly. "Can I walk with you guys?"

The girls stared at her. Then they glanced at one another.

"What, they let you out of jail already?" Augusta demanded.

Jodi smiled. She wondered if Augusta was joking. For some

reason, though, all she could really think about was how beautiful Augusta's blond hair looked.

"Um, I don't know how to get to Kappa Kappa Gamma," Jodi said.

Augusta sneered. "Good," she snapped.

Augusta and the other girls walked away from her.

Jodi shook her head. "I don't get it," she called after them. "Have I been blackballed?"

"As *if*," Augusta said. She didn't bother turning around. "To be blackballed, you have to get as far as being asked to rush. And you haven't."

It took Jodi nearly two hours to find her way home. She spent most of it crying. The pill was definitely beginning to wear off. All she wanted to do was go to sleep and pretend the night had never happened. But when she opened the door to the triple, she found Ali and Celeste waiting up for her—and her bed burnt to a crisp. The mattress was little more than a blackened slab. Her sheets and blankets were long gone.

"Oh my God," Jodi said.

It was almost funny. Clearly Jesus was not on her side. No, it appeared that if anybody was on her side, it was Satan. What a night! She had made a fool of herself in front of Zack, she had been rejected by the one place where she really thought she would have a home (Kappa Kappa Gamma had been her last hope), she had no bed . . . and now she was face-to-face with Celeste. Wonderful. Just wonderful.

Ali and Celeste stared at her. They looked scared.

"What happened?" Jodi asked.

"Lazy-eyed, narcoleptic K. J. Martin fell asleep with the hot plate on," Celeste said.

Jodi hung her head. "I see. So. Where am I going to sleep?"

"Here," Celeste said.

Ali and Celeste stepped aside to reveal a small cot, made up with nice clean sheets and Celeste's comforter.

"The firemen brought this over from the infirmary after they put out the blaze," Celeste explained. "You can sleep here. Or, no—you can sleep in my bed and I'll take the cot."

Jodi didn't say anything.

"I'm so sorry about fooling around with Buster," Celeste suddenly blurted. Tears began welling up in her eyes. "Jodi, please. I'm so sorry. I was so drunk, and I didn't even know what I was doing, but that's no excuse and I shouldn't have even been talking to him in the first place. You have to forgive me. I don't blame you for getting so mad. It was really awful of me to do whatever I did with him, even though I don't remember what it was. I haven't talked to him since that night and I promise I never will again—"

"Stop," Jodi interrupted. She held up her hands and shook her head. She couldn't deal with this right now. She felt terrible and guilty and mean, and yes, she was sick of fighting—especially since the fight involved her shitbag of an ex-boyfriend . . . but still. After what she'd been through tonight, a heart-to-heart was the last thing she needed.

THE ALPHABETICAL HOOKUP LIST

Celeste sniffed. "So that's it? You're not going to accept my apology?" She looked pleadingly at Ali. She was *really* sorry. She'd never been more sorry about anything. *Ever.* Not even when she accidentally tossed out Jib's entire fall harvest with the garbage, thereby destroying nearly twenty-five thousand dollars' worth of marijuana. (Although in all fairness to her, he *had* put it in an unmarked trash bag.)

"Jodi," Ali said. "Come on—"

"Look," Jodi interrupted. "I didn't say I wasn't going to accept the apology." She smiled sadly, remembering the conversation she'd had with Zack in the library. "I mean, I overreacted. The truth is, I have no idea how the whole thing happened. I didn't let you explain yourself."

Celeste's face turned red. "I got drunk. I know that's no excuse, but I guess I was just out of control. You know?"

Jodi looked at her. She swallowed. Yes, she *did* know about being out of control. She'd been so out of control a mere three hours ago that she'd wanted nothing more than to throw Zack down on the dance floor of a Christian rave and have sex with him right there. She shook her head. That was not the way adults acted. Adults learned from their own and others' mistakes. Adults were empathetic. Adults forgave their friends. . . .

"I should apologize, too," Jodi whispered. It was hard to speak. Her throat felt tight. "It's my fault our whole dorm almost burned down due to my incredible stupidity in lending our hot plate to a lazy-eyed narcoleptic."

"A lazy-eyed, narcoleptic pyromaniac," Ali added.

"I'm sorry, you guys," Jodi said. She sniffed. Her eyes were watering.

"I'm sorry, too," Celeste said.

The three of them were silent.

All of a sudden Celeste jumped forward and hugged Jodi.

Remarkably enough, Jodi found herself hugging back. Maybe she was more of an adult than she'd realized. Because she *could* forgive Celeste. Or she could start to forgive Celeste, anyway. Even though she'd known Celeste for about one percent of the time she'd known Buster, she already knew that Celeste would never, ever betray her like that again. Or maybe she didn't *know* it for certain. But she had a feeling. And it was a good one.

Besides, if Celeste *did* betray her like that again, Jodi would be forced to kill her.

"I'm sorry, three," Ali said, joining in the hug.

Jodi stepped back. "What do *you* have to be sorry about?"

"I'm sorry that I'm whipping your asses so badly in the Alphabetical Hookup List!" Ali exclaimed, breaking their embrace. "That is, if you're still in it with me?" She couldn't wait to whip out her list and show them she was up to *K*.

Celeste and Jodi grinned at each other.

"I'm in," Celeste said.

"I'm in, too," Jodi said quietly.

There was a loud knock on the door.

The girls frowned. Who could possibly be banging on their door at three in the morning?

But then a thought occurred to Jodi. Zack had come

looking for her. Of course! She darted to the door and threw it open.

It wasn't Zack. It was some chubby guy with a crew cut and a bowling shirt. The name *Dirk* was stitched in script on the breast pocket.

"Can I help you?" Jodi asked, annoyed.

"Jodi Stein?" he asked.

"Yeah?"

"I help out with security in the mail room. I know it's late, but we found your packages and I wanted to get them to you right away. All you have to do is come with me and sign for them. We got a truck waiting to help bring them to you."

Jodi smiled. "Really?" She was suddenly more ecstatic than when she'd been on Ecstasy.

"Dude!" Ali cried.

"Hurray!" Celeste chimed in.

Jodi turned and winked at her friends. "Dirk is a great name," she said. "And you know what?"

"What?" he asked.

"Dirk begins with *D*."

"Wow, you freshmen *are* smart," Dirk said.

Jodi grabbed him by the pocket of his shirt and kissed him.

Ali and Celeste looked at each other and laughed.

"Whoa," Dirk muttered once she had finished.

"You know what?" Jodi said to Ali and Celeste. "It feels like the first day all over again. Only better because I have my stuff."

"And we've got each other," Celeste said.

"And we've got the you-know-what, too, dude," Ali added.

"Yeah, *dude*," Celeste said, laughing.

"Yeah, dude," Jodi added. The three of them hugged again. They hugged for a long, long time.

It was only later that morning, as Jodi twisted and squirmed in the cot (no way was she going to let Celeste sleep on it— the bed burning was entirely *her* fault), that she realized something. Or maybe she'd known it all along, and she hadn't accepted it. Sort of like the way she'd never accepted that Buster wasn't right for her. But this realization . . . it was a pretty big deal. Especially because she couldn't tell her room-mates about it.

Kissing Dirk had been sort of an act. Kissing *all* those boys had been an act, with one big exception. She hadn't been as out of control as she thought. No . . . now, stone-cold sober, with the sun beginning to rise, she was finally coming to terms with the truth. The Alphabetical Hookup List was going to be a big problem. Because she didn't want to kiss anybody at all, except for one boy. And his name started with *Z*.

More on the way...

The Alphabetical Hook-up List

An all-new series

A–J
K-S
T-Z

Three sizzling new titles
Coming soon from
PHOEBE M<u>c</u>PHEE
and MTV Books

www.mtv.com

www.alloy.com

Like this is the only one...

Floating
Robin Troy

The Perks of Being a Wallflower
Stephen Chbosky

The Fuck-up
Arthur Nersesian

Dreamworld
Jane Goldman

Fake Liar Cheat
Tod Goldberg

Pieces
edited by Stephen Chbosky

Dogrun
Arthur Nersesian

Brave New Girl
Louisa Luna

The Foreigner
Meg Castaldo

Tunnel Vision
Keith Lowe

Number Six Fumbles
Rachel Solar-Tuttle

Crooked
Louisa Luna

More from the young, the hip,
and the up-and-coming.
Brought to you by MTV Books.

POCKET
BOOKS